Earl Rasnov's
Bloody Soirée

A novel by

Paul Riedel

Earl Rasnov's Bloody Soirée

von

Paul Riedel

www.paul-riedel.de

Printed in Germany

First edition 2018

Second Edition 2020

Bibliographic information of the German National Library: The German National Library registered this publication in the German National Bibliography; detailed bibliographic data are available online at www.dnb.de.

Cover: © Paul Riedel, Munich 2016
Editor: Michael von Sehlen

Translation: Ailsa McKillop

Production and publisher

BoD – Books on Demand, Norderstedt, Germany

ISBN: 978-3-7519-9808-6

The Author

Paul Riedel is a name which has been recurrent in my family for many generations. You could suppose this family to be short on imagination when it comes to naming their new-borns; however, you would be mistaken!

We are a family where creativity for baby names is handed down from one generation to another.

We had an art historian, an editor, a technical draughtsman and now me, in the current generation, as an artist and computer scientist in our family.

This shows that all Paul Riedels stayed true to art, directly or indirectly. As I don't have any sons, this line of Pauls will end, unless one of my sisters changes my prophecy—wonders never cease. All of my ancestors had, besides their art, another career going on.

I was born in Brazil where I grew up under a mixed upbringing which included knowledge of mixed ethnicity. I saw black ghettos where people believed in Umbanda, the Brazilian pagan belief which originates in Africa.

I explored the strict Catholic background of my Italian ancestry. From my mother's side I learned about her Neapolitan and Umbrian foundation to the Lutheran origin coming from my father's side. I developed a comprehensive vision of belief and reality.

Preface

When I started writing at the beginning of the eighties, I was caught somewhere between many influences of wild love of the seventies and the young rebels, as we called them in Brazil. Today, I'm aware that being twenty means still being in a phase of self-discovery. All of this together led to me having such a broad sense of creativity with several exhibitions where I showed colourful pictures, which are still part of my artistic journey.

It took me a few years longer to start writing, as it always seemed harder for me to find the words in which I could describe what I saw. This encompassed the language of technology, emoticons and immature Anglicism or fashionable, changing expressions and obviously the perceptions of people.

During this story I refer to one of my first concepts: a small group of actors and murder. Back in the day, several friends of mine died from the battle against AIDS. They were diagnosed with pneumonia, immunodeficiency or even cancer. No one wanted to face the truth and say what illness it actually was.

Sexual freedom was, and still is, a problem. What I took from this phase of my life, however, is that there are many actors who try to portray the life of a stranger, just as if it were theirs. Prejudices are why we don't meet new people and why we don't develop further in life. Those fears, which we express as belief, tradition and conviction, become some kind of blindfold which keeps us from seeing all those possibilities the future could hold for us. What is special about those people who try so hard to work against those standards and regulations, is not only their ability to act like others, to show us how other people suffer, but also to hide their own characters.

It could be they don't actually know themselves how they feel. And even if they do, they hardly know that these feelings are not part of a personalised character.

This book contains insights into my experiences from my time as an actor and from all the groups I could work with. I hope the story shows how I personally gained so much from those people.

And now I will hand over to Earl Rasnov and his ensemble.

Earl Rasnov's invitation

The sun had already set and left only a glimmer behind in the sky. An uncomfortable coldness made its way into the bedroom of Natalia, a thirty-four old daughter of an Italian family. Her graceful and romantic temper was hidden under the veil of depression today. She felt like she was too tired to get up and too tired to fall asleep.

On her old clock from the nineties she could see one of the numbers flickering. It was hard for her to read what it actually said.

'I have to get up,' Natalia tried to convince herself, but she felt too tired to even try.

She pushed up her hips, which were slightly too wide, and the bed made a warning noise as her weight shifted. On the wall was a poster of herself as a graceful dancer in a variety. Today this picture looked like a dream which could've been true a long time ago. On the small table with the clock was also a sealed purple envelope which had big letters on it. They looked like they had been made by spider which took a bath in ink and had a lot of fun while dancing those letters out on the envelope.

The heavy pollination gave her immune system a hard time. She hadn't been able to move properly for a few days and now she had a migraine as well.

Once her bum had found the right place in bed, she reached over to get her reading glasses. The phone rang, distracting her from thinking about how much weight she had gained.

She lifted the receiver.

"Grossbeck!" she announced, slightly too fast and a bit too miserably, while her glasses fell to the floor. "Damn!" slipped out of her mouth.

"Oh dear, what's wrong with you? Why did you say damn? You didn't even ask who it was that called you. So …" A heap of accusations came from the other end of the line, but she was used to her husband talking to her like this.

The last time they had talked was already two weeks ago and it almost felt like she was answering the call of a stranger.

"What's up, Otto?" She was slightly annoyed when she interrupted her moaning partner. Natalia bent over the edge of the bed and reached down, trying to find her glasses again.

Otto was a few years older than she and more successful than her acting career with his music business.

The small pause he made between her question and her moaning on his end of the phone indicated what this call was about.

"You're *still* not coming back home?" she asked slowly and made sure to emphasise that this wasn't the first time this had happened.

"No," Otto admitted, slightly ashamed.

"What kind of company is this? They make you fly around the globe without a plan as to when you'll come back? When are you going to come home?" Natalia realised that they had been having this same discussion every week for almost a year.

"I booked my flight for Friday, so I'll arrive at eight p.m.," Otto whined, and it was obvious that Natalia made him feel defensive.

She picked up her glasses and resumed her old position, ignoring the warning noises the bed made.

"Last week you said the same thing in your email. You told me you'd come back today. I'm looking forward to seeing if this time you'll actually return on Friday. What's wrong with you? Don't you want to come home?" She knew herself how unnecessary this question was. It was simply a cry for help with no sign of a response.

She could hardly hide her disappointment. Otto stayed away most nights, as he took on jobs from a big company where he had to arrange shows in several cities. He seemed to make good money, but their private life suffered a lot. Otto had married her when she announced she was pregnant.

"We can talk over the computer," whined Otto.

She looked at the envelope and put on her glasses.

"Rasno sent us a letter," Natalia said, holding the phone between her shoulder and her ear.

Rasno was short for Rasnov, or, as he liked to call himself, Earl Rasnov. He was an acquaintance who liked to invite them to a special event every year. He was also the producer of the variety show where Otto had met Natalia for the first time.

"Rasno? Ah, Earl Rasnov?" Otto had a teasing undertone in his voice. Everyone knew that Earl Rasnov had never been an actual Earl. It was the name of a character from a circus at the beginning of the twentieth century. During these shows, the character proved adventurous and mediumistic skills. Earl Rasnov took on his name and cherished his ancestors on many posters in his theatre. They showed pictures of him in magical blue gowns with tight trousers in black and red or horrific purple, with a face so white, it could easily have been mistaken for the narrator of a horror show.

"Obviously, Otto. What else do we call Rasnov?"

"What's the occasion? Is it the anniversary of his daughter again?"

Less than three years ago, Earl Rasnov's daughter, Elmira, had died in an accident on stage. Natalia had ended up with minor injuries when she tried to save his daughter.

Natalia had already ripped the envelope open when she saw that there was a dedicated side to open it. She had accidentally damaged the side of the letter. Her small fingers groped for what was inside the envelope and she pulled out a card.

"I ripped the side of the letter, damn it!" Natalia was irritated with herself for having ripped the beautifully decorated card.

"What does he say?"

"Wait. There's a lot of paper in here," said Natalia while she spread out tickets and a voucher for a hotel in front of her.

"Well, okay – so?" Otto urged her.

"Ah, okay. It's an invitation to a soirée. He sent instructions for what we should prepare. The song you once wrote … blah, blah blah … wait. Hmmm? He wants me to dance. Apparently, he's forgotten that my leg is not as pretty as it was, but I'm sure I can manage. Okay, tickets are included, as well as travel documents – wait, what?"

The last words sounded more like protest coming out of her mouth.

"What's wrong?" asked Otto. He was now even more curious.

"Separate rooms. But we're married. That's rubbish. We'll change it as soon as we're there. We will get paid as well. Well, when all's said and done, it was his daughter. We really can't cancel on him, can we? He will also present his new show and I could really do with the money." This question was not needed, as Natalia needed the money from Earl Rasnov and Otto got all his offers because the Earl recommended him everywhere.

"I really don't know why he has to call his afternoon teas a soirée." Natalia had never understood that this word was also part of the German language and in all the dictionaries she never opened. She wasn't too interested in foreign words and malicious tongues said she wasn't very good with German words either.

"Natalia, my dear. It's a reception in the evening and not just afternoon tea. That'd be called *début de soirée*. Leave it now." It wasn't the first time Otto had explained it to her. Every year she was confused when they received Rasnov's invitation.

"Please go ahead if you want to treat me like a fool. But I know it's called zoarrey as well," she said in her own French version. Otto just ignored her and continued the conversation.

"He invited us; what's the date? Tell me, so I can put it in my calendar. I'll have to talk to my tour manager." Otto never argued with the way Natalia perceived things, nor her interpretation of more sophisticated vocabulary. He knew that it was just a waste of time. She soon forgot his explanations. Sometimes he thought about how close Natalia must be to a fish, as they always forget everything immediately as well.

"Don't be such a smart arse! Is a *Tourmanager* not some kind of German football position? I will send the date to you as a text message. We have to go. I really need his recommendations and his money. I don't have many students, and once the current courses are over, I don't know what to do anymore. I think, in case we get another bad summer like the last one, we might have to close the school. I just don't know what Rasno wants to do with the part his daughter owned. I can't give him the money for it."

There was an unexpected noise on the other end of the call, and it made Natalia suspicious. It wasn't anything in particular, but there was something that got her attention.

Otto inhaled deeply. Apparently, he wasn't very interested in the problems she had with her dancing school. He just didn't know how to end the conversation.

"Sorry, I'm tired." Otto sounded like he wasn't even listening to Natalia.

"Is there someone with you?" Natalia asked, feeling slightly jealous, as she couldn't stop herself from asking.

"No, I'm watching TV. I'll call you tomorrow. I have to go to dinner now and then I'll go to bed." Natalia could hear someone pouring a glass of water. Again, she wanted to ask who was with him in his room. However, as soon as he finished his sentence, he hung up on her. He just mumbled a goodbye, which was cut off mid word by him pressing the red button on his phone. She was hurt and convinced that Otto was cheating on her.

She looked down at the carefully written invitation and pressed the envelope against her bosom. The alarm went off and reminded her that she had to be at the dance school in one hour. As always, she would have to smile and pretend to be a successful dancer for one hour.

✦

Otto was on his bed in his hotel room in Hanover. His voice sounded off as he rested his hand on his throat when he hung up. He threw the phone on the bed and looked in the direction of the fridge. A man, who was almost two metres tall, was pouring himself a glass of water.

"Don't make such a noise when I'm on the phone. I can't stand those outbursts of jealousy and I'm sure she'll ask me for money again." Otto repeatedly pushed the red button on his phone, but the screen looked like it was waiting for something else.

The red-haired man was in his underwear and sat down on the edge of the bed. He didn't look too guilty with the glass of water in his hand, which he had poured while Otto was on the phone to his wife.

"I just wanted to drink something." Pavel raised the glass with his other hand and pointed at it while faking a burp.

"And if you were any louder when you burp, I would've thrown my phone at you." Otto enjoyed the way Pavel teased him.

Pavel was a contradiction in himself. He was tall, very big and hairy like a bear. At the same time, he acted like a child; he was funny and very charismatic. Nothing seemed to be threatening about him when he smiled. But his strong hands could make people talking to him feel intimidated. Pavel put the empty glass down on the desk in front of the bed, jumped towards Otto and pulled him towards his warm body.

"I know you like it when I burp loudly and provoke Natalia." Pavel laughed at his own joke. Otto pulled a face and the disgust he felt for noises like these showed.

"I'm serious. Don't cause any trouble. As soon as she finds out about the two of us, she'll sue me for everything I own. And if you're not careful, she'll sue you as well. Mental cruelty or something. She already mentioned something like it." Otto put his phone aside and let Pavel push him to his side. He enjoyed the feeling of closure and how tender Pavel's big hands felt.

"Otto, eventually we'll have to stop hiding. Natalia is not that stupid. She'll realise that you're not spending all those weeks at your shows. I might be your assistant, but eventually she'll realise that we're sharing a room. What did you talk about? What kind of invitation?"

Otto led Pavel's hand towards his chest and indicated to him to undo his shirt. Pavel did what he wished for and his beard touched Otto's small neck. He could smell the woody scent of Pavel's freshly washed skin and he soon forgot about the conversation.

Over the last few years, Otto had lost a lot of hair and his face showed the stress Natalia caused him.

His face was wrinkly and pale, instead of fresh and young and as soon as he put on his glasses, he looked even older and more resigned.

Pavel traced his hand gently from Otto's belly button up to his neck and took off his glasses. They had been dating long before Otto got married and when Natalia announced her pregnancy, Pavel started to suffer from a horrible depression.

"Earl Rasnov has invited us to one of his soirées again. His daughter Elmira has been dead for almost three years now. I think he wants to socialise again and the last time we were together was when Elmira died. I will definitely have to go to this. I even get paid this time."

Pavel only listened with one ear. He gently tried to take off Otto's work clothes.

Their bodies pushed aside the cold hotel duvet and it made a rustling noise when it fell to the floor. Soon, Otto's clothes landed next to it.

"You were his musician and I'm sure you'll have to go. But definitely not without his comedian. Don't forget that it was me who got most of the applause. I'll have an invitation once I get home as well."

Otto was still thinking about how he'd leave Natalia to continue his life with Pavel. He wanted to quit playing hide and seek and wished he could finally be proud of their relationship. Natalia put too much pressure on him, and he couldn't handle it anymore.

"Sure," Otto tried to say while trying to escape from one of Pavel's kisses.

"We've been dating for more than four years now. Don't you think we should finally stop this farce? I don't want to hide and be scared of Natalia all the time. She's busy handling her school and I know that she'll get over it. I still don't believe that she was pregnant anyway. I don't believe it. Not back then and not today. As soon as she told you she was no longer pregnant, you should've left her." Pavel threw Otto's ripped jeans onto the pile on the floor and looked concerned when he faced his lover. His Ukrainian accent was charming, and his baritone voice sounded soothing. He didn't keep it a secret that he was only interested in same-sex relationships; however, Otto wasn't out yet and was scared to lose the few friends he had once their relationship became public.

"Money is just one problem. The other one is that Natalia wants revenge and I'm sure you don't know what you signed up for. You don't know what she'll try once she knows about us. She can just tell everyone about my past, simply to seek revenge."

"Darling. She's so stupid, no one actually listens to her when she speaks. I have to admit that many of my own jokes are on her account and the things she once said. She's just a fountain of stupidity. For example, she once said that Oscar Wilde was a composer on Broadway, and you were friends with him. I don't think the mushroom growing between her ears actually contains anything like a brain. I'm sure there's just a sign saying, 'For hire'. But let me tell you, Oscar Wilde once said: 'Blessed are those who don't have anything to say and just shut up.' And she asked when I heard him say that, but yes, she's really just a silly girl."

Pavel spoke slowly and gently, but he sounded like he was on stage. He was always funny and sometimes very mischievous. He didn't keep it a secret that he couldn't stand Natalia, but always made it sound like a joke. While Pavel tried to distract Otto from their conversation, his libido woke up and he didn't worry about anything else anymore.

"Don't be so rude. I admit, I don't know why I actually agreed to marry her. But it'd cost me a fortune to get a divorce now."

The last bit of clothing on Otto offered no resistance and Pavel's big hands pulled Otto's body towards his chest. His long and curly chest hair felt like an inviting and warm blanket and Otto stopped fighting those cuddles.

"She's a liar. No, she's a stupid liar. She claimed to be pregnant, just so you'd marry her. Just because of this lie you should've left her, to move in with me."

Otto pulled the duvet up from the floor over both of them and thought about his situation. He couldn't keep his relationship with Pavel a secret anymore and he just had to divorce Natalia.

"Don't you think Ignez will be at Rasno's event as well?" Otto asked, caught in his thoughts.

"I thought Ignez was busy with an exhibition in Lyon. She sent me a postcard together with the invitation. Unfortunately, I couldn't find anything online about it. Must've been something private. I'm sure she'll have received an invitation as she's part of the core group of Earl Rasnov. I bet he's planning on producing another show with us if he invited all of us to see his soirée. Ignez might be a good painter, but she rarely sells her art. I'm sure she'll be happy about the new season with Rasno. Why? Do you think she could help you with your divorce?"

"It's just a thought, but I know that Ignez hates Natalia just as much as you do and once she told me that if I ever wanted to divorce her, she'd help me out. It's something you don't discuss over the phone. I wanted to talk to her about it last year already, but Natalia was with me the whole evening and I didn't get the chance to speak to Ignez. You two get along very well."

"Sure. I was the one who recommended her to join our group. I've known her for more than ten years now. Do you want me to call her?" Pavel got rid of his very last piece of clothing and threw it to the floor.

"Could you ask her if she got an invitation as well? And please let her know that I want to talk to her. I'm thankful for every bit of help I can get. Should we go and get some food now?"

Pavel traced Otto's arm and ended in his hand. He then pulled it towards his warm, inviting genitals and whispered hoarsely: "Now? Food? Are you sure?"

"No. Maybe in half an hour?" asked Otto.

"Let's say forty-five minutes," murmured Pavel and finished off his sentence with a teasing kiss.

✦

White walls, covered in paintings, vibrated because of the loud screams from a forty-year old crying woman. Her black hair was long and touched her hips. It was all around her gentle face and made her look like a character out of a horror film. She scrunched up a tissue and threw it with all her rage towards the floor. Quickly, she got out another tissue from the box on the table and continued screaming.

"Dear, don't cry. It was just a stupid exhibition. Who could've known that it was fraud?" A woman with greying hair, Catalan dialect and a dark voice tried to calm her down. Benta used to be a professional soprano with her own shows in the variety shows of Earl Rasnov. As expected, her voice changed with her age, but she could still reach all the high notes. She was the reason why Rasno's shows were sold out. People loved her Spanish aura, which gave her a more noble appearance on posters and on stage.

Her daughter was a very unlucky person. Ignez walked into every trap she could find. She was a good, but definitely not exceptional painter, who used to design the concepts for Earl Rasnov's stage and paint it during the florescence of his variety shows. After Elmira died and when Rasno stopped the show, she tried to get through life with one exhibition after another. During the last three years, she'd had people cheat on her, steal from her and use her, and now a woman called Natalia stole from her.

Natalia tried to be a good agent, but there was definitely room for improvement. This time, it included a lot of trouble and expenses.

"They gave me an award and claimed to pay for every single one of my paintings. I put so much money into this, and they promised me to give back twice as much." Ignez sounded almost like a Swabian now. She concealed her Spanish origin under the veil of integration. Another paper tissue landed on the floor and she was even more in a rage when she pulled out the next one.

Ignez went up and down, her heels damaging the oak-coloured floor. Benta rolled her eyes towards the sky and took a deep breath in.

"You don't have a copy of your paintings, no picture, not even a document of delivery. I'm sorry dear, but I didn't pay for your expensive training for you to do something as stupid as this." For one moment, Benta lost her temper.

Ignez got up again and forgot to cry for one second. She grabbed the tissue, made a fist and pointed it towards Benta. Benta loved her daughter dearly, but it took a lot of strength to endure her outbursts as the drama queen she was. She knew that for the next three weeks this would be the main topic, and every time Ignez would come up with an even more evil way to seek revenge, which she wouldn't let go for hours afterwards. Sometimes she was scared that her daughter would actually follow up on those threats.

"Mother? What camera am I supposed to use for those pictures? I don't even have a phone and those awards seemed trustworthy to me. They'll all have to pay. Especially Natalia."

Although Ignez was so unlucky, she lacked neither motivation nor anger. Her black hair flew around her head and made her look quite creepy, as if she would soon put a curse on the world and transform into a demon. Even Benta, who was used to outbreaks like these, got the chills this time.

"You now know that the award was just fake, and the agency doesn't even exist online. They cancelled their website just three days after you left. What did you do in that time? Why did you not realize that there wasn't an exhibition?" asked Benta. She was shocked at how naïve her daughter was.

"I just trusted that I'd read everything more carefully this time. It looked super-serious and Natalia convinced me completely. Now my pictures are somewhere in Switzerland and everything I did in the last six months was for nothing." Ignez wanted to prompt Benta to feel sorry for her and presented everything even more emotionally. But Benta just lost her temper again.

"Enough now! You're naïve and careless. Something Natalia recommends is never anything you can base your business on. That's a common fact. Especially because you don't even like her. Why did you listen to what she said? She's an even bigger drama than you and your business. We have to focus on the future now. Earl Rasnov contacted us. Every one of us. This year, we'll get paid. He wants me to sing for him. He wrote down some songs, but I think this year I have a new one for him. He'll like it. And you're supposed to design the stage the exact way it looked like when his daughter died. Cruel. But as long as he pays us …" Benta was so honoured she almost rolled her eyes towards the sky and touched her chest, looking very ladylike.

Ignez blew her nose which didn't sound as ladylike as hoped. As soon as she went to throw away the dirty tissue, her eyes met the warning look from her mother. Ignez snorted and put the tissue on the table.

"I see. Earl Rasnov wants to hear you sing. Do you think Natalia knew about what those traitors did to me?" asked Ignez in an undertone.

The wavy dress, made of fancy chiffon, followed every movement, which made it look like it would fly behind Ignez. It was the most expensive gift she had received from Rasno at the time when she was working for his variety show. Ignez was a woman of much jewellery and accessories and there was always something dramatic about her appearance. She was slightly more composed when she thought about her chances of getting back all the money she had lost at this fake exhibition.

"I'm sure Natalia knew about it. There's nothing I would put past her. I could bet that she received some kind of provision for your simplicity. This bitch might be just as stupid as a pile of hay, but she's smart when it comes to her business. *Hija*, you'll never get your money back. Even if you could prove they stole all your paintings. Natalia is broke. She had to pass on the money she got from you immediately. She's in too much debt. I'm sure everyone knows about it."

Ignez continued to go up and down the room and her Spanish roots became very obvious. Since both of them had moved to Germany, they tried their best to integrate, but they couldn't deny their roots. Even without Benta's dialect, it was obvious that both women were proud and determined Spaniards. Ignez put both her hands to her hips and raised her chest.

"I'll make sure she'll feel the consequences. This was the third time I believed what she said. Every time it was just another fraud. I'm done with her. I should've told everybody about how she seduced Frederik and went back to Otto where she faked her pregnancy." Her beautiful dark eyes were still sparkling while her look changed, and she asked calmly: "What exactly did Earl Rasnov tell us?"

Benta thought that it was slightly weird how Ignez just changed her moods, but she got out the invitations and read them out loud.

"'You're invited to join Earl Rasnov's bloody soirée.' He sent train tickets and a voucher for a hotel in Eschenlohe. I don't even know where Eschenlohe would be." Benta got out her tablet and looked for it on her route planner.

"Where is it?" asked Ignez. She was caught in her own thoughts and touched her chin.

"It's in the South. Lower Bavaria, isn't it?" Benta never understood the difference between South and Lower and Upper Bavaria.

"No, that's Upper Bavaria if it's in the south. Did anything else arrive today? I'm expecting a parcel."

"No, but Pavel called. If I understood correctly, he wants to take you out for some food. I wrote down his number, but I never understand what his Ukrainian shirtlifter has to say. He can't speak German, although he's been in Munich longer than the two of us together. It's embarrassing how he pronounces the name of Earl Rasnov. Every time, I think he sneezed or needs to cough. 'Raash'!" parroted Benta.

"Mother, please. I don't even want to hear you criticising the way he talks. He's more Russian than you and if he pronounces a Russian name like this, we should be the ones learning from him." Her warning looks didn't show any effect on Benta who just ignored her. "You shouldn't call him a shirtlifter either."

"But he does get changed in the women's changing room, doesn't he? He's tall, but hmmm..." Benta pointed towards her crotch and laughed.

Pavel's size was a common topic which all women liked to talk about. He showed his genitals to everyone without any embarrassment whatsoever, so every comment in the group was aimed at him.

"Please, mother. I really like Pavel and I feel comfortable around him. He never cheated on me, nor did he steal from me like your hetero girlfriends. I don't care who he's into, about his comments and his … size …" Both women laughed loudly and Ignez sat down next to her mother. She read the invitation and looked at the tickets and vouchers.

"I'm looking forward to seeing all of them again. I'm sure Frederik and Bianca will be there too." Ignez seemed to be a lot calmer now.

"I'm not too sure if it's the best idea to have Bianca and Natalia in one room together after Elmira died. They despise each other," Benta said chattily, just like she usually did.

"Frederik had something with every woman in the group. Even with you, but we always respected Bianca," Ignez explained.

"How do you know? We're just good friends, the other part of the story doesn't necessarily have to be true," said Benta, slightly offended. She adjusted her hair, as if the topic didn't concern her at all.

"What does Elmira's death have to do with both of them?" thought Ignez.

"Actually, not much. But it was this day when Bianca realised that Natalia had something with Frederik. Natalia should've just got dressed and left the caravan, but she wanted to take on the role of being the new lover. Bad luck. Normally, women don't like anything like that, do they? Frederik submitted like a dog." Benta loved to gossip and she told the story every year. But every time she tweaked it slightly by changing the emphasis and point.

"Right. Apparently, it was just a caravan thing, not a real affair. Just like all the others. That's how I understood it. I wasn't interested in the problem back when Bianca came screaming out of her changing room and met Natalia. It really was scandalous. But it's a good time for me to find like-minded people. Natalia will suffer for this. Do you have Bianca's phone number?"

Benta got up and closed the living room window. The cold evening air seemed wetter and it made her shiver.

She got out her tablet again and looked though it until she found a page with every address.

"Mother. You're just brilliant. So organised. Thank you. I don't need Pavel's number. I know it by heart."

Ignez got out her phone and noted all the numbers. Once she was finished, she looked at her mother and smiled.

"I just came up with a great idea. *Gracias*, mother."

Shelves with hundreds of books covered the walls. Small, big, old and new books were piled on top of each other with no order. Although it looked more chaotic than the interesting method of Frederik van Marwijck to keep it all tidy, it was still obvious that he was a very clean person. He had an eye on everything and it was more organised than in any other usual home.

He was always aware of a harmonic colour and style when it came to buying his own clothes. It was important for him that all his clothes looked good together. You could say he was a dandy, and every woman was fascinated by him. That was a fact he was aware of.

No matter if he was dressed, or not.

Since the accident on stage, when he held Elmira while she took her last breath, he had suffered from a trauma which he tried to overcome by taking his mind off it.

This time, his books were his therapy. He brushed them and got the vacuum cleaner to get rid of the last bit of dust.

The postman rode his electric bike past his window and braked loudly.

'Working days. The postman only comes on working days.' Frederik organised his thoughts.

He didn't want to stop working because of the postman. If he did, it could cost him a whole hour to find the right position where he could clean his books again.

"Bianca!" he shouted and waited for a minute until he could continue his work.

'Mail has to be picked up in person,' the voice inside his ear warned him.

"Damn it, Bianca. Where are you?" he shouted. He was very annoyed now.

'One, two, three. Who knows how many letters there are if no one picks it up from the door?' another familiar voice whispered in his head.

He was confused why Bianca didn't answer and he made some noises to show how unhappy he was; however, there was no one around to hear them.

It looked like his broad shoulders and his slim body had collapsed under the curse of the voices inside his head, but it was still obvious that he was a very attractive man. Once he went outside his library and into the hallway, Bianca rushed towards him.

"Go back into your library. I was just on the loo!" she said to him. She sounded like she was out of breath while she pulled down her skirt.

"It's your fault that I have to start this row again!" Frederik acted like a child and went back into his library.

Bianca just ignored him and thought that it must have been because of his age. Two years ago, they had celebrated his sixtieth birthday, and since then he had started getting weirder and weirder. As soon as the postman arrived, she had to go to the door, count the letters and bring them inside. She found comfort in the memories of all the years they had spent together. Frederik was almost ten years older than she, but for whatever reason, the last six months had made him age quickly and it looked like he had lost his original happiness. Frederik wrote most of the shows for Earl Rasnov and he received awards from other institutions as well. Bianca was concerned about the state he was in, but she never brought it up because it always caused trouble. It got louder and louder and more painful every time.

Bianca knew that he wasn't over the shock he had suffered three years ago, and together with other problems, his symptoms got worse.

"Rasno sent us a … wait …" She opened the letter and left the remaining mail on the desk.

"Mail we receive belongs in the blue basket and not there. Otherwise we could confuse it with old mail we already dealt with. Don't be so sloppy," he warned her.

Bianca took a deep breath in and recited her daily mantra: 'It's just a phase, it's just a phase.'

"Well? What's it about?" Frederik checked the vacuum cleaner twice, to make sure it was working.

"Oh dear! He wants to invite the whole group. He's such a good host. He wants to perform 'The bloody soirée'." She skimmed through the letter, thought about something for a second, turned on her phone and looked at the calendar.

The 'Bloody soirée' was a show which Frederik had written several years ago and which combined dance, poetry and singing with the more infamous characters from horror stories.

"Awkward. He invited us just for the weekend we wanted to go to Vienna. However, we won't go there because we have to see all the others. Oh, it'll be great. Pavel, Otto, Ignez … !" cheered Bianca.

'The bloody slut will be there too, and she'll tell everyone how bad you are in bed,' sneered a nasty voice in his head.

"Shit. You forgot Natalia. Elmira was the one who died and not this stupid woman." Every time Frederik got angry, his hands would start to tremble and sometimes he got incontinent. Bianca looked at him and wondered how far it would go this time. "Do we really have to go? Maybe I'll call and ask him not to invite this horrible person."

Bianca quickly laughed and shook her head. She gently took his hands and put them on her chest. She knew it would calm him down. Despite the condition he was in, she still enjoyed his hands and tried to fight the tears which came creeping up. She successfully managed to hide her feelings.

"That's news to me. When I found both of you in the caravan, I was sure there was at least one part of you which was really into her." Her shiny eyes accompanied her gentle smile and she pointed towards his penis, which was in Natalia's hands back in the day.

Frederik had to laugh. Over the years, a lot of women tried to seduce him and even a few men tried their luck, although they were never successful. He was aware of how sensual and attractive he was. Sometimes it caused an argument, but Bianca could cope with it. A few days of sexual retreat and he wouldn't pull a face for the next few months. That's how she had controlled him over the last thirty-five years they had already spent together.

"You're not still angry at her because of that, are you?" he asked charmingly. He wanted to put away the vacuum cleaner and hug his beloved Bianca, but it felt like the apparatus was cursed and seemed to control his mind. He couldn't let it go.

"Never. I just think she doesn't fit into our group. A cheap woman like her can act like she was one of us sophisticated women for a certain amount of time, but she should never forget where she actually belongs. Poor Otto who was naïve enough to believe her. I don't think he could actually make a child." Bianca sounded weirdly noble and acted as if she was better than any criticism. She kept it a secret, but she hated the fact that a woman as young as her had something with her husband.

"Why? She seduced him. He's young and probably able to make a child. It's no surprise if a woman gets pregnant," said Frederik, sounding like a know-it-all.

"Fred, please. He's with Pavel and thinks no one knows. He's naïve and she needed someone who could support her financially. Otherwise she wouldn't have picked you either. You're one generation too old for her." Bianca knew more about Pavel's relationship than Frederik realised.

"Right. You told me. I don't know how a guy as small as Otto can handle it. I don't feel comfortable with hugging a man as big as Pavel. Imagine a bear like him coming even closer to you. I think Otto can be glad that Pavel didn't squeeze him yet." Frederik's hand stopped trembling.

"Pavel is so gentle. He couldn't ever hurt anyone. He's just tall." Bianca really liked Pavel.

"But lonely. Otto decided to be with Natalia," said Frederik.

"I don't think so. Pavel is on his side during all his shows. I just wish Pavel would do what he actually wants."

Frederik finished hoovering the last books and put them where they belonged.

"Right division, organised by name of the author, name of the book and, in this case, edition." He was excited by his organisation.

"Darling, sometimes you really scare me. When will you finally finish here?"

"There are four rows left. If I lose count, I have to start again. But I have a system." Frederik pointed towards the rows which he had already cleaned. In Bianca's opinion, they all looked the same.

"Ah, I see, hmm." Bianca wasn't quite convinced, but she wanted to avoid any kind of argument.

Frederik realised that he should hurry and hoovered four books at once to finish the row.

"I'm sorry, but I have to finish it."

"Yes, Fred. If I were to worry about every one of your girls, I wouldn't have any hair left. Don't worry. I will not work with a cheap woman like her. What do you think is Rasnov's plan? We haven't heard from him since his daughter died. I sometimes thought he wouldn't be in touch ever again.

"What happened to his daughter shocked us all. I occasionally think about how bad my own trauma must be." Frederik had been there when the accident had happened.

'Dance, dance, jump and step,' whined one of the invisible voices in his head.

Elmira and Natalia and were to perform a synchronised dance, while he was supposed to go to the centre of the stage to present the show.

'Legs up and turn,' recited the voice and laughed loudly.

He tried to remember what he would have liked to forget. For three years he had tried to forget about this moment, but every time someone mentioned the women's names, or he just thought about the variety show, the memories came back and the ghosts of his past tortured him.

'Arms forward – and bend,' repeated the voice three times. He wanted to bend down, but there was some rationality left in him which stopped him.

He looked ahead and the crowd gaped. The main girder crumpled silently.

'Continue, I say.'

He suppressed the noise and concentrated on the audience. Both beautiful women stepped forward and the audience cheered while they were dancing.

'*De coté*!' ordered the voice.

Two half-naked women turned on their delicate feet and their veils flew around them like a spell. The noise from the girder repeated itself; this time it was louder. Still Frederik ignored it. Helena, the conductor, signalled something from where the orchestra was, but Frederik just thought she was joking.

'*Écaré devant.*' His memories showed both girls stepping towards the audience with one leg forward.

When he heard the noise for the third time, he couldn't ignore it any longer and it ended with the lights falling down. They hit Natalia's leg and tragically ended Elmira's life.

'*Plié*!' ordered the voice even louder.

"Frederik!" Bianca shouted and shook his shoulders.

'*Tombe.*'

The construction made a horrible noise when it fell on both dancers and hit Elmira's head. Natalia had jumped over to her to help when the second part of the construction hit her leg.

The memories stopped and everything turned black. He felt dizzy when he woke up again and his heart was beating heavily in his chest.

"Love, I think I have to lie down."

"Leave the books. We'll go into the living room and I'll call Helene and Virginia. By the way, Ignez called as well. She asked me to call her back, but I was in the bathroom. Please, be careful with the step."

Both of them entered the living room and Frederik started trembling again. Bianca tucked him in and gave him a kiss. She was close to crying when she thought about the time when his illness would take him away from her for good.

Frederik fell asleep much faster than expected. Bianca took the wireless phone and went into the kitchen. She pushed the buttons carefully and listened attentively in the direction of the living room.

"Ignez?"

A female voice mumbled happily on the other end of the call.

"Darling, how much I miss you." This time, Bianca couldn't suppress her tears anymore and they came, together with a sad adagio.

Suddenly, she remembered how Ignez had stood there after the accident and said: "The wrong one just died."

Being a smaller woman was definitely a big advantage. That's what Virginia thought when she looked at her new dress in the Biedermeier mirror in the room. She pulled the new dress until there weren't any wrinkles in it anymore and pushed her left leg forwards. Virginia had been used to being in the circus ring since she was only a little child. Her parents were part of the circus in the seventies. For many years they refused to have a permanent residence. Virginia was trained by the best people in the business and she showed everyone how flexible she was when she performed as 'Marva – the snake woman'. No matter what it was, dancing or juggling, she always managed to leave the audience breathless when performing with her knives or torches. Her eyes weren't the best anymore, but she was always confident of not missing a target ten metres away when she threw a knife.

"Bianca wrote that Frederik's not well," said Helene thoughtfully from her desk.

They had never got married but had lived together for more than five years. Helene was responsible for the wardrobe and she could create a beautiful evening dress for a magician out of just two pieces of fabric.

"Thank you, Helene. This dress is beautiful. What's wrong with Frederik again?"

Virginia was more interested in her dress and didn't even turn her head while talking to Helene. She put her other leg to the front and made sure it didn't have any wrinkles again. The dress had green sequins in demanding arabesques on it.

"Bianca sent us an email which said that she was concerned about Frederik's health. Apparently, he has a lot of blackouts and recently he became compulsive, she said. A man as beautiful as he is! Hard to believe. He was definitely the most handsome man we ever had in our shows. But that's life. Don't you think I should emphasise my hips somehow?"

With heavy steps, Virginia went from one side to the other and watched herself closely in the mirror to make sure the dress didn't throw any wrinkles.

"Not if I have to kneel down and I'm not planning on it. My arse looks beautiful in it. You're a real artist. Frederik never recovered from the shock he had after Elmira died. Rasno wanted to convince him to see a psychiatrist, but Bianca didn't agree. I hope she can at least agree now that Rasno was right. Very sad, all of it."

Again, Virginia went from one side to the other in Helene's small workshop. She tried to make long steps in front of the big mirror to see how that would change her look. After Helene watched her for a while, she turned around to her.

"Please could you shorten it a bit here? My legs are too short for this amount of fabric. No one can see my legs there. If I step to the side, I'd look like a snail." Virginia arched her back to emphasize her snail look. Helene laughed patiently and noted Virginia's next wish mentally. She was used to her extra wishes and knew that she always wanted to look perfectly. Virginia wanted to look just like the star her reputation said she was for the upcoming reception Earl Rasnov invited them to.

"I will, but if I shorten it more than two centimetres, you would have to wear the dress as a necklace. I'd especially have to make sure not to cut through the sequins. I'll change it but I can't shorten it anymore. Rasno wants us to arrive earlier than the others, as I have to have a look and check their dresses. In the event of Natalia having put on even more weight, I might have to skin an elephant to get enough leather. It easily could've been twenty kilos she put on last year, wasn't it?"

Virginia stood in front of the mirror and was proud of her hair and make-up. She put her hair up and watched how it transformed her. In her opinion, it didn't look too good, so she collected all her hair on the right side and made it look slightly bigger.

"Fat? I thought she might've eaten the dancing instructor. Oh dear, what a ton she was. That's something that'll never happen to me. I don't want to wear my hair as a bun. I'm done with buns. Did Rasno write the invitation himself or did he instruct Benny to do it?" whined Virginia.

"I don't know, but everything is hand-written. I think Benny learned calligraphy. Rasno's not as good at writing with a feather," said Helene.

"We'd all be screwed without Benny. He's so elegant and nice. I just wonder why he gets along with Natalia. But, oh well. What should I do with my hair?"

Virginia tried another version where she put her hair up. It looked like Shockheaded Peter could be jealous.

"But you can't juggle fire when your hair is free and I'm sure you don't want to wear your knives as a hairclip, so a bun is the only way to go. Don't be so girly. Buns are great and you don't have to dye your hair. Bianca replied to my email and said working with Rasno will help Frederik to get out of his depression. I don't want to get involved, but I think it's more likely for him to snap when we're all together. He was really close to it last year." While Helene was talking, she juggled two needles between her lips.

"True. I almost forgot about it. It looked like he got weaker every time Natalia looked at him. This woman manages to make everyone mad. I think, besides Earl Rasnov, no one can actually stand her. And we really have enough reasons. I would've really liked to hit her when she said that she didn't like dogs and kicked our baby Hugo." Virginia loved her Jack Russell, Hugo, even more than herself and she'd never have a performance without him. A few years ago, Hugo's father died peacefully and Hugo took on his part of the show. He wasn't scared at all and hunted everything that Virginia ordered him to hunt, no matter if it was fire or knives.

Helene just shook her head because of how Virginia exaggerated. She knew that it was better to ignore most of it. In her opinion. Natalia hadn't kicked Hugo on purpose, but rather by accident.

Hugo lay in his basket and sighed. He probably wanted a bit more peace in the room. While Virginia tested throwing invisible knives around, Helene looked at the contours of the dress she was making.

Virginia went to the jewellery box made out of pearl which an Indian prince apparently had given to her. She was looking for something she could add to complete her outfit.

"My red knife-shaped earrings are not in here," she mumbled.

"Darling, I do design costumes, but I surely don't wear earrings like these. You don't have to ask me where they are. Natalia fell out with everyone and not one of us would like to see her again if it wasn't for our love for Rasno. I think he finally noticed that as well. In my opinion, the biggest problem is that she's too stupid and extremely arrogant. She once said that the top of her feet hurt, and I told her it could be that she had tendonitis. She just replied saying that she doesn't type on her computer with her feet. Apparently, she only knows tendonitis on her hands, what do I know? She's really someone special. I don't like her because she always thinks she's someone better and I don't like the way she treats me. And, of course, she still owes me money." Helene didn't want to be resentful, although she clearly was.

"Pavel also said he'd rather kiss everyone's arse before he'd open the show by dancing with her. I'm sure the silly girl didn't even realise what Otto is up to," chatted Virginia secretively.

"It'll all go wrong. I'll text Rasno and tell him not to make us work with her. I'm definitely not doing the opening dance with her either. She's too annoying. Ignez would be perfect for it. By the way, she always said that she was from Italy, but she clearly doesn't have a clue about the country. She always confuses Sardinia with Sicily and she barely speaks a word of Italian." Helene got up and put one of the needles which waited between her lips into the new hem of Virginia's dress.

"Enough now, love. Take the dress off and let me change it for you. I'll call Frederik later. Maybe it'll brighten him up and he might feel better. We've always been good friends." Helene was slightly surprised that she hadn't heard from either of them for a long time now, but she could understand the situation after hearing the news.

"Do you think he'll have to go to psychiatry eventually?" Virginia said from beneath the dress which she was taking off.

"Well. If nothing else will help him. Bianca has to continue to live her life and Frederik will not get any younger. It's a hard situation to be in. If it's okay, I'll go and get our suitcases out of the basement and we'll talk through your wardrobe for the stay at Earl Rasnov's."

"Yeeees," said Virginia, while Helene left the living room. "But this time, I'll make sure Natalia will end up where she belongs." Her small, shiny eyes looked like a vindictive fairy who had just found a victim.

✦

There were receipts, notes and many other office supplies on the desk which he should probably organise at some point. Benny, son of Earl Rasnov, was trying to find a comfortable position by sitting with one foot on a chair and the other one tucked under his bum.

He'd sent out all the invitations and everyone had got back to him already, confirming that they'd come. However, Benny wasn't done with his tasks yet. Trying to read his father's handwriting didn't make his job easier.

"Dad. Come here again, please. I really can't read your handwriting," Benny complained.

Earl Rasnov was his stage name, but it was his real name to him. His old name, Peter Lutzow, was part of his past and he would probably not even realise it was his if someone called him. Benny and Elmira were his children and the only things left after his beloved wife died. He then said goodbye to Peter Lutzow and took on the name of Earl Rasnov. His wife had died of lung cancer when Elmira hadn't even started school. Benny, who was slightly older than Elmira, suffered for years from the shock of losing his mother.

On Benny's desk were pictures of his family and two smaller, silver frames with pictures of his mother and Elmira.

Since Pavel introduced Earl Rasnov to Benta seven years ago, they had got closer. However, nothing could ever substitute the closure of the past between Rasnov and his wife.

His father hurried to him, put his head on Benny's shoulder and pushed his glasses into the right position.

"You shouldn't claim your father has bad handwriting. That's very rude." It was a well-known trait of Earl Rasnov to have a strong sense of pride, but Benny just ignored him.

"Maybe it's the handwriting of one of those ghosts in your head," joked Benny.

"Sure. If I remember correctly, it was an honourable Scribes of Pharaoh Hatshepsut, whose ghost is still wandering around on this planet, as she murdered her son." Earl Rasnov gently pushed his son's neck.

"Dad," warned Benny.

"Oh, what shall I do when you finally get married and leave me back in this house? Well, let me see. Umm??? It should be … Yes. The technicians of the theatre should check the lights and this time, I want them to check them again during the meeting with the actors. I will present my new show and I don't want them to be reminded of the accident. It took me a long time to get over the shock. I'm sure you too." Earl Rasnov started to tear up as he smelled his son. Suddenly, he saw all the memories of his son, who was there for him even during the times he had to suffer through the loss of both family members. He suppressed his feelings, but it was more often now that he got the feeling of eventually being alone.

"You're still afraid another accident will happen. Eventually we'll have to let go. Accidents can happen. But enough now. I'll write an order for the technician of the show who will look after it," said Benny.

"And you're sure everyone will be there for the show?" asked Earl Rasnov.

"Yes, Dad. I checked it five times already. No one will cancel and even Natalia will be there, although no one likes her." Benny let his glasses slide down his nose.

"Poor Natalia. I think it's only Virginia who can actually stand her."

"No, apparently Frederik likes her veeeery much." Benny emphasised the penultimate word at great length, until his father gave him a little slap on the back of his head.

"Don't say anything like this in front of your mother." Earl Rasnov still thought that the ghost of his wife was around him. Benny wasn't too keen on imagining things like that, but he respected his father. He simply thought it was funny, what had happened between Bianca and Natalia.

"All right, Dad. I'm sure even mother would've found it funny," laughed Benny while writing an email to the electrician of the stage.

"You're right. I think no one thought it was embarrass-ing except me. You better make sure to stay away from her. The only reason I invited her was because she's still leading the dancing school and a friend of your sister. And I don't want to lose her as the agent of the group, but apparently our finances aren't right." Earl Rasnov pointed at the screen and showed his son where he'd made a typo.

"I would've seen it, Dad. I also have a correction program. Don't worry. But it'd be better if you didn't invite Natalia. I'm scared everyone will still be mad at her. And she didn't send us the bank statements." Benny sent the email and the computer acknowledged it by making a beep.

"Did Helene receive the manuscript with the instructions for the costumes? She's the most important person of all."

"Sure, Dad. You already mentioned it a few times. Don't be so nervous. Everything will be just fine. We'll just have to be patient. It's a big group and a few of them are busy with other things. We don't even know if our research was right. I still have a lot to do with how everything will go down. That you picked the 'bloody soirée' didn't make it any easier for me either. You have to admit that Frederik sent other really good concepts as well." Benny was old enough to lead his own group, and his father seemed to look forward to his son taking over the business.

"The inn in Eschenlohe prepared everything already. I was just on the phone with them."

"Dad, that's what I did this morning as well, just like you wanted me to. Go outside in the garden and lie down for a bit. You make me nervous. It'll be fine, you'll see," reassured Benny.

"Okay, well. I want Helene to check my costume as well. All right, I'll go to the garden."

Earl Rasnov was sulking and went to the garden. He felt useless. Benny could manage everything without him and the only thing that was important for him was to get some rest. The upcoming days could be the end of his variety show.

✦

The taxi drove slowly on the busy streets of Schwabing on its way to the train station. On the back seat sat Natalia, who had just dried the sweat off her forehead with a tissue. Her heart was beating heavily because of how excited and exhausted she was. It didn't make it any easier for her to carry four suitcases, but she didn't want to send it via special delivery like Benny had recommended her to.

As expected, Otto hadn't come home from his travels and he had promised her to pick her up at the train station in Eschenlohe. He was planning on being there two days before her and thought it would be less stressful to meet her there.

As Natalia got out of the taxi, the driver looked deeply into her eyes and waited for a positive reaction. It took Natalia a few seconds to realise finally what the driver wanted from her.

"I'm sorry, but my suitcases are too heavy for me to get them out of the car," she said in a teaching tone, trying to sound very ladylike.

The taxi driver moaned and got out her suitcases. He hoped she'd realise it was appropriate for her to tip him now. However, as soon as he bent down to pick up her suitcases, she waved a porter from the train station to come to her. Her suitcases were lifted onto a trolley and she paid by card. The taxi driver vainly waited for his tip.

"Cheapskate," he mumbled.

"What did you just say? I don't have time for you. I have to go to a presentation. Please follow me to Platform twenty-two." She performed her own version of the famous dancer Isadora Duncan and walked in front of the railway assistant. She indicated for him to follow her.

He also just got a simple 'thank you' and she got onto the train, hoping that she hadn't lost anything.

"Can you tell me why I have to go to Garmisch-Partenkirchen first? I want to go to Eschenlohe," moaned Natalia to the porter, who was out of breath already.

"Eschenlohe is on the way. It's before you reach the final stop," he said.

"They really could explain that better, couldn't they?" She threw herself onto the seat she had reserved and ignored the angel who had just helped her with her luggage.

She tied her own backpack up with a leather strap which she had appropriated from their last show. It was the handle of the trapeze where dancers hold onto the ropes.

Natalia got her travel documents out of her bag and went through them again. She didn't like something about how it was written, but she couldn't pinpoint it.

She took out her phone and tried to call Otto. After it had rung for a bit, the voicemail answered. She opened her documents and read them through.

Earl Rasnov seemed to have kept his fashion sense. He wanted to have the exact same things they had worn three years ago. She'd have to tell Helene to make it a bit bigger as she had gained more than twenty kilos.

She read Benny's ornamental handwriting with hints on the printed hotel reservation, as well as on the travel plan. So far, she couldn't find anything out of the ordinary. There weren't any hints for the dancing school either. However, the advices to the financial records of the school and the last orders of the artists made her feel slightly uncomfortable. It put her in a bad spot, as she'd wanted to take the opportunity to ask Earl Rasnov for money.

She had been on the train for three hours already and she was tired when she got a text message.

She just remembered Earl Rasnov's instructions which stated that she'd get the main role on stage this time, and not Frederik.

'Well, he certainly is not the youngest anymore,' she thought.

Natalia realised that Earl Rasnov finally must have seen more in her as he had given her the role she waited for.

"But who should dance behind me, Earl?" she cursed in an undertone and no one in her compartment understood what it was about.

The victim

Someone loudly pulled the curtains and opened the window in a bedroom in Munich. A dull noise came at the same time as an unexpected breath of fresh air and although he was sleepy, Otto saw the outline of his lover.

"I already sent my bags to the hotel via courier, as well as your other ones. We just have to take these two backpacks." Pavel was checking the bedroom and sounded busy while he talked without looking at Otto directly. From the first moment when Pavel woke up, he was hyperactive, most probably because of the alarm clock playing music from the sixties.

Pavel's big head was oiled and shone proudly in the sunlight. His red hair made him look almost like a Nordic god. Otto couldn't enjoy much of the beauty of his lover, beyond the moments they spent together. Unfortunately, there was still one hurdle to overcome and he told himself to do it soon. Thinking about his wife Natalia put a downer on his mood.

He didn't want to risk the beauty of the moment and say something wrong, so he threw his duvet aside and jumped out of bed.

"All right, I'll have a bath. Will you make breakfast?" For the brief moment he lost his composure, his voice sounded slightly quavery. He almost sounded like a small boy calling for his mother.

Pavel drew artistic figures in the air and pushed his heavy body into the wardrobe.

Whenever Otto stayed at Pavel's, he mostly slept without any clothes on and that was how he got up. Pavel quickly looked at Otto's silhouette, which looked unreal in the light which shone into the room. Otto didn't have many muscles, nor did he in any way have as much masculinity and thus nothing to talk about. However, his graceful body showed a sense of romanticism which helped him to thrill the audience.

Otto came into the bathroom while Pavel got out his waistcoat with the sequins. He held it in front of his big chest and checked whether there was just a tiny bit of fat on him.

"I feel like I have to be sick," he said in a deep baritone. Pavel checked both sides of his costume and saw that the adornments were about to rip on some parts.

"I can't hear you!" shouted Otto from under the shower.

Pavel ran into the bathroom and heavy, dull steps on the floor followed him while he said hectically:

"I paid a fortune for this." He pointed towards his blue and black waistcoat. His chest looked a lot bigger in it and the fire of his fiery tassels on stage mirrored in the sequins which left the audience speechless.

Pavel was already seeing a picture in his head, of himself on stage, losing all his clothes until he stood there with just a nude thong and the audience would boo him. Those tragic pictures of a costume falling off his body made him shiver.

"It's a catastrophe. How am I supposed to play with fire in a garment like this?"

Otto turned off the water and fished for his towel through the opening of the shower.

"What's wrong? I want to have some breakfast," moaned Otto under his towel.

"It looks like the seams are starting to break." Otto pulled at a few of the broken parts of the costume.

Otto was familiar with moments like these and he tried to act rationally.

"I'm sure Helene will be able to fix it. Or you could go on stage naked. I'm sure the audience would be very happy."

"Silly!" snorted Pavel and turned around towards the living room. "I'll call Helene. You'll make breakfast," ordered the giant and was determined when he went to the phone.

"I have to get dressed first," said Otto, who felt like he wasn't being treated very nicely.

"You don't have to be dressed to make breakfast. It'd be even better if you weren't," laughed Pavel with the phone held to his ear. He lifted a finger to his lips. "Hush now, it's ringing."

Otto wrapped a towel around his waist and went barefoot into the kitchen.

"Helene?" Pavel asked feverishly. "Helene, my darling. It's Pavel." It wasn't very necessary of him to tell her, everyone knew his voice, just as his dramatic undertone, and everything else really.

"Hi Pavel. We're running late with packing. What's up?" Helene's voice sounded a bit off and Pavel was scared that she wasn't in the mood to listen to his problem.

"I'm sorry, dear. Could you please bring your glue gun? Rasno wants me to be the fiery djinn during the rehearsal. I read his script and every one of us should be a character from a horror story. Mine is the one of the djinns. I wanted to wear my blue and black waistcoat, but it seems to be falling apart."

Helene didn't seem to be in the mood to talk, and before he could continue his rant, she interrupted him.

"Yes, I'd have brought it anyway. I'm the wife of Frankenstein. I have to take a few tools for the rehearsal. Throw it away. It was just too cheap. I told you already when you bought it," Helene sounded like a friendly teacher with a harsh undertone.

"Well, the designer's name is Franco Antonionni and it's not from Asia made by poor children. I can't believe it. How am I supposed to act as the djinn? Did

Rasno lose his mind? I'm too tall and I could at least be Earl Drago with my waistcoat." Both of them laughed, as it was obvious that he was making a joke about Rasno calling himself an Earl. The joke was based on Rasno not really being an Earl. "Rasno is getting very senile now. He must've confused me with someone." Pavel looked worried and turned from one to the other side in front of his mirror. His face looked worried, although there was no reason for it by the look of his body.

"I won't say you're the prettiest now and please, stop moaning at this time of the day. A man as tall as you are …" Helene stopped talking abruptly as she already knew which joke would follow. "I don't want to hear anything about your dick. Okay, I'll bring everything with me, but we're rushing here, sorry. We'll see each other tonight anyway. Virginia wants to go to Munich before we go, and we'll buy a few things Rasno ordered us to."

Helene hung up so quickly, Pavel couldn't even say goodbye properly.

He was disappointed when he went back into the kitchen where Otto was still wrapped in his towel trying to create breakfast for both of them.

"Please, no Eggs Benedict. They're disgusting." Pavel pulled an ugly face.

"It's Bianca's recipe. The French are well-known for their cooking talent. I don't understand what you don't like about it," said Otto while the water was boiling in the pan.

"Bianca is from the Czech Republic," corrected Pavel. "Are you sure I can still go on stage in this?"

"Pavel, my love, you're worried for no reason. You could go on stage with only a body painting on and no one would realise because of the bad lighting. Did you talk to Helene?" Otto opened the window to let the steam of the Eggs Benedict out.

"Yes. She said she could repair it. But what are those girls doing in Munich at this time of the day? It's not even seven o'clock." Pavel went into the hallway with his waistcoat and Otto could hear him packing the torn thing into a plastic bag.

"I don't understand why we have to be awake at this time of the day. Normally, we're not up before ten o'clock." Otto served plates to both of them and sat down at the higher kitchen table.

"I wanted to pack the car on time and arrive there at three o'clock, just on time. Benny asked me if I could help him."

"That's not a problem. The problem will be something else. Natalia will not be happy, and we have to be prepared to face this confrontation." Otto talked with his mouth half-full and one of his eggs burned his throat.

"Come on! Don't eat like a horse. I'll handle Natalia." Pavel knocked his thumb on his chest and laughed. He knew he was the only one out of the group who Natalia couldn't fool. He fought a long fight to have the man he always wanted back.

He looked tenderly at his Otto and took a deep breath in. He was ready for any fight it needed to defend his love.

Meanwhile, Otto received a short text message, but neither of them cared.

✦

Steam and dirt filled the air and it looked like the flat had been empty for a few months. The pictures on the wall showed performances, which indicated the semi-success of the residents on stage. Helene stood in front of one of them pictures she had received as a present from the group. It pictured the best costumes she had ever made. She was obviously very annoyed when she hung up the phone.

"What was that?" asked Virginia sulkily. She was sitting on the make-up table in the bedroom. She looked at her brown hair which she had now styled a bit more voluminously. She tried to conceal how annoyed she was by her partner's behaviour by doing her hair.

"Pavel. He has another torn piece of clothing. He really should learn how to fix his own things." Helene had black hair and was French. Sometimes it was hard to understand her accent, especially when she was in a bad mood.

"Ah, him again. A man as tall as him and still he's moaning so much. But it doesn't matter. We love him." Virginia was happy with what she had done to her hair and looked at it in the mirror.

"I could do with a bit less attention, but it's okay." Helene judged Virginia's work.

"Why are you so cruel during the last few weeks? I didn't do anything, did I? It's hard to be around you nowadays. What should get less attention? Do you want me to become a nun? Well, you've definitely been more charming before."

Helene lived in her own world, and neither friends nor relatives could understand it. She looked down on an open envelope on the table and was especially interested in the change of date for an upcoming project.

Faithful Hugo immediately realised the change of mood in the room and went to the living room. He had had to witness their arguments a few times when they threw everything around the room. Today he didn't want to be in the audience.

Virginia knew that they didn't get along as well as they did four years ago. Helene seemed to be more confused.

Helene left the room and didn't want to hear anything anymore. Virginia didn't like arguments and always tried to avoid them, but apparently it gave her a bad feeling thinking about another season on stage together with her moody partner.

Virginia read through Frederik's scripts which Earl Rasnov sent and thought about how she could be the woman with the axe. She was small and petite. Of course, she could always aim with knives, but throwing axes, she had to admit, was probably better for Pavel.

'But I look a lot better in a corset than Pavel.' She quickly laughed at her own joke.

Helene left the workshop and called someone in the living room. Virginia was scared that this time there was more on the table than just her performance at Earl Rasnov's new show 'The bloody soirée'. She decided to act in a bit more of a confrontational manner this time, because she had to think about her performance, no matter if it was with Helene or without. Despite any kind of love, she knew that her work came before anything else and she wasn't ready to have problems in the next season because of Helene.

Quietly, she went into the living room and tried not to give the impression of listening to what Helene said. It was slightly too obvious when she stroked Hugo and acted as if she didn't realise Helene was on the phone.

"Sure, I'll be there. I was just about to leave, but as I said, I have an appointment this afternoon and I can't cancel it. I therefore wanted to make sure you didn't forget about this meeting." Helene sounded very professional and her French dialect was barely noticeable. She tried really hard to speak good German.

"I understand," mumbled Helene.

'What's up?' thought Virginia and grabbed a glass of water, which she left forgotten on the table earlier.

"Yes. You're right."

'Damn it, where is it?' Virginia acted as if she was looking for something in her dresser while listening to every word of the conversation.

"Okay. I'll be there in twenty minutes." Helene hung up and looked at Virginia surprised.

"Oh God, don't look at me that way. I'm just looking for something in this dresser. I wasn't interested in your conversation at all."

"*Oui, ma chère. Je suis folle.* I have to go. We'll meet at the station at three o'clock." It was obvious that Helene wasn't in a mood to talk and Virginia tried to conceal her failed attempt to spy.

"Sure, sure. Well, I'm busy as well. Hmmm ..." As this didn't show any effect, she added "Where are you going?"

"Will you be okay to get the suitcase there by yourself?" Helene sounded cold and there wasn't any hope for an answer to the question.

"Wait. What did Natalia do to you that you're so cold? I asked you to forget about this job in Berlin.

Recommendations of Natalia are useless. I thought we agreed on it." Virginia did everything she could to talk to Helene, but it looked like Helene had other ideas.

After Elmira died Earl Rasno made Natalia head of the dance school and the agency of the artists. Natalia did a decent job for a few months, but for a few weeks now there had been many problems with the artists.

"Virginia, it's not all about the things Natalia did wrong. I just got the job from Natalia, but it's the manager of the theatre who wants my work and Natalia has nothing to do with it anymore." Helene seemed off during the last years of their relationship and everything changed more into a flat share.

Although Helene wasn't interested in Natalia for long, it had a bad influence on their relationship.

Natalia tried to save herself from the ruins by acting like an agent and handing out bad jobs to members of the group, which caused a lot of trouble.

"Sure. Just go. I'll be fine. I'll take Hugo for a walk now." Hugo understood immediately that it was time to go for a walk. He stretched his front legs and yawned charmingly. "See you later," said Virginia in a quite sad mood.

Less than one minute later, Helene was out of sight and Virginia was disappointed. She looked at herself in the mirror and had a hard time trying to hold back her tears. She got out the bag for Hugo's walks and went to the door. Hugo followed her like a shadow.

'I hate you, Natalia.' Virginia pulled the leather band so tightly around her hand, the blood stopped flowing in her veins. Her hand turned red and she cursed the day when Natalia came into their lives.

✦

The breakfast dishes were organised neatly in a maisonette in Schwabing. Judging by the ingredients, the Spanish ties were obvious. A middle-sized woman in her flannel dressing gown sat at the table and played with one hand with the flowers on the place mat.

"Ignez, my dear," came from the other end of the phone. Frederik sounded slightly guttural. "I'll set off for the train station soon. Bianca left earlier; she said she'd have to pick up a few drugs from the pharmacy. How are you and your mother?"

Ignez got up and went to the door where she stopped between three suitcases and one backpack. She tried to watch the time while being on the phone.

"I was just on the phone to Virginia. She's out with Hugo. Why are you in such a rush? Your train doesn't go until the afternoon. Virginia and Helene are the first to go. If we're too early, we'd have to take a taxi to go to Eschenlohe. Benny doesn't want to drive twice. He clearly wrote it in the invitation." Just like her mother, Ignez knew how to be determined and she always talked in a bossy tone to her friends. She threw herself onto the green sofa and exhaled loudly.

"I don't usually call Virginia. What did she say?" Frederik was the second one in the group and always tried to take on the role of being a good father, even if it caused arguments between him and Earl Rasnov sometimes, because he was just slightly too nice to women.

Ignez went into the kitchen while talking on the phone, got a pot of coffee and poured herself a cup. The living room was in a state and their upcoming trip converted even the last bit of organisation, which Benta treasured so much, into pure chaos.

"Cortado?" asked Frederik, who was familiar with the things his colleague liked to do.

"*Si, mi amor*. I really need it right now."

"What's up?"

"Helene got a job from Natalia in Berlin. Can you believe it? This bitch who stole my pictures still tries to make business and we'll all go down with her. I don't understand how Helene could listen to her. Apparently, Helene tried to become more independent from Virginia. Since the accident, they didn't seem as peaceful as they were when I met them."

The smell of coffee and milk came out of the cup and Ignez waved it towards her face.

"You do the Cortado just like your mother. What trouble did Natalia cause for Helene?"

"It looks like the advance payment for a contract is missing, or it's not enough. Well, it looks like Natalia doesn't have any money," summarised Ignez confusedly.

"Bianca prepared everything already. I'm just sitting here waiting for a taxi. Until then I'll watch my afternoon shows on TV. Don't worry about Helene. She'll soon realise that Natalia just is who she is." Thinking about Natalia always made Frederik shiver.

"You're as good as ordering people around as Rasno. What's your role in the 'bloody soirée'?"

Frederik looked into the blankness and thought about what his role was. He didn't seem to know. Those blackouts happened to him more often these days and it was really hard on him.

"Well … Rasno wants me to play a warlock, a male witch, and at the end, I should dance the succubus together with Pavel. I'm sure it'll be a lot of work and the choreography will be challenging. We could use a lot from the last show. The question is, whether Rasno realises that I've got a bit older. If your mother is dancing as well, turns and splits will only be possible if she's on ropes." Ignez laughed, thinking about her flying mother who was lifted into ropes.

"Strong ropes," she added.

"Don't let your mother hear you. She's still skinnier than Natalia. Oh dear, how much weight she put on!" Frederik quickly lost his train of thought and made a short, unnoticeable break before he changed the topic. "Where was Virginia?" Frederik distracted her to gain back his memory.

"Well, Natalia is still home, and she told me about the job Natalia arranged for Helene. I didn't want to get involved, but I told Virginia about my cancelled exhibition. She was furious and attacked Helene for weeks. She tries to convince her not to work with Natalia. I listened to her, but I didn't want to get involved. We'll have a lot to talk about when we're all in Murnau. Natalia will have to be prepared." Most of the time, Ignez was more reserved and didn't want anyone to know what was going on in her private life.

"Oh shit! Once Natalia has someone tied up into her business, she can be very stubborn. She's not the smartest, but definitely determined," added Frederik.

'It was this horrible bitch who should've died,' said a squeaky voice next to Frederik.

It made him jump and he made a quick noise.

"Did something happen, Frederik?"

Frederik's hands where trembling and he wasn't sure if Ignez heard the voice as well.

"Oh, nothing. I just … spilled something. Go on." He covered up his insecure voice by sounding overly excited.

"Virginia went out with Hugo for a walk through the pedestrian zone in Munich. She wanted to go shopping before we leave. I'll send her a text. Maybe she'll meet Bianca in town," explained Ignez and forgot to look at the time.

"It's not even nine o'clock. They'll catch a cold out there. I'm sure Bianca sits somewhere at the market and thinks about how she could present herself during the new show. During moments like these, she's always rather alone." Frederik looked around and regained his composure once he realised the voice was just in his head.

"How will Virginia perform after she caught a cold? I don't want one of her knives cutting us in half. Being Rumpelstiltskin isn't part of the show." Ignez raised her hands towards the sky, as if she were asking it for protection. Frederik could hear her voice being further away from the phone now.

'Snip, snap, bang and boom,' laughed the devil and his voice made the whole room shake. Frederik felt dizzy and forced himself to sit down.

"Darling, I have to lie down for a moment. I think I didn't get enough rest last night," apologised Frederik. He suspected someone of turning on the radio somewhere.

"Sure. I also don't want to talk about accidents. Since what happened to Elmira, everyone is scared to perform all those great tricks on stage. I have to check if everything I ordered is on its way to the theatre in Murnau already. I think it'll be enough for the rehearsal. I will decorate everything with lights so we can save the costs of moving and we won't need as many staff as normally." Ignez didn't stop talking and Frederik was just waiting for her to pause so he could say goodbye.

"Wait, Ignez. My programme just started. We'll talk later," said Frederik. He was grateful for every pause Ignez made to breathe.

"Okay, see you later," said Ignez.

The room around Frederik seemed to float, like in the Devil's Wheel, a carousel which was traditional in Munich. When he was a child, he had enjoyed going there once a year. However, right now he wasn't too happy about it.

He got a text message and he suddenly got up and finished his cold coffee in one go.

Don't forget to take your pills. They're on the kitchen table, texted Bianca.

'She caught you. She spies on you," the ghost tortured Frederik again.

"No!" Frederik screamed desperately.

'Ignez doesn't believe you.'

✦

The train station in Murnau seemed deserted and there were just a few empty bottles of beer and energy drinks decorating the surroundings. An old man, dressed in clothes from the seventies, collected them with a resigned look on his face. He looked at the three men standing in front of the big bin, until they moved and let him pass.

"Are you sure she got the right instructions?" the tall man named Pavel asked.

"Sure. My father asked me the same question for the whole week already and I never disappointed him. But you can't forget it's Natalia we're talking about here. Maybe she'll appear in thirty days because she went on a trip to Japan." Benny laughed and sent her a text message to find out where she was.

The man put a few bottles into his shopping trolley and looked at them to make sure they wouldn't chase him away.

"I'm sure she just took a later train, or, like you said, the wrong one. What should we do now?" Pavel was nervous as Otto had promised him to solve the issue with Natalia tonight. But if she didn't come, he'd be caught in this nightmare he'd had for three years, for another night.

The man shuffled through bins and selected cans and bottles.

"The train will be here in a minute and Ignez and Berta will be on it as well, if everything goes as planned. I wanted to make three journeys to pick everyone up, except you and Otto. I wanted to take you separately. We have to catch up on a lot, don't we?" Benny poked Pavel, who faked his whining and laughing. Apparently, it was a private gesture between both of them. They also wanted to make the time pass.

Just as they hoped, they could see the train just in front of the city with only about ten minutes' delay. They could clearly hear the signal of it from where they stood above the main street. The train braked abruptly, and the tracks made a loud noise on the old platform. Everyone who was waiting for someone on the train just stood there, cursing because of the delay. There was an apology coming out of the speakers, but it could barely be heard because of the noise of the train. No one was interested in it anyway.

The man who collected the bottles sat down on a bench and looked at the three men waiting for their friends.

"Look for Natalia, Ignez and Benta. Maybe Natalia will be on it as well, because she's running late," Pavel said to his boyfriend.

"I hope she didn't come up with any stupid ideas. My father was already so nervous, he could've started flying," said Benny, slightly out of breath.

They went along the train and there alighted a woman, in a red and black dress, and with hair no one could miss. It was Ignez, who just asked her mother to hand her the suitcases. Pavel and Benny ran to help out.

Everyone was happy to see each other and there were a few kisses, just as was the tradition in Spain, before Benta got out the luggage.

"Oh God, what is it that women have to carry around?" asked Pavel. "I just have my backpack."

"We're not planning on spending our days naked just like you. Cheap thing, you! Did you bring your Otto?" Ignez smacked Pavel's arse and looked for Natalia behind him.

"Pssst. Natalia is on this train as well. I don't want her to find out like this," warned Pavel and continued to look around.

"Natalia? On this train? I would've seen her. It's a short train and I went up and down twice because I had to stretch my legs," said Benta. "No, she wasn't on this train."

Pavel looked at Benny and shrugged.

"We'll go. She won't arrive here today after this. I'll check the planes to Japan. Wait …" Pavel suddenly turned around to Ignez.

"You didn't throw her off of the train, did you?" he joked.

"Don't be silly. I'm sure it'd be great if no one was watching, but I wouldn't touch her, not even with tongs. She's not worthy of my revenge. I just ignore her." Ignez lifted up her chin to emphasise how disgusted she was.

"Yes. Benta already sent me an email that something went wrong with your exhibition. I'm sorry, dear. You should've asked me. I'm an expert in Natalia's recommendations." Pavel had had to make several annoying experiences with Natalia's recommendations as well.

"Call her. She has to hear her phone, doesn't she?" asked Benta. She sounded slightly worried. Despite what Natalia did to the group, she was still part of it.

"I wouldn't worry. We're talking about Natalia here and she always finds a way to manage." Benny carried all the heavy luggage over to Pavel and together they went to the car park. The smell of urine, old beer and other indefinable spices covered up the smell of the lilac.

Suddenly Benny's phone rang loudly, and he put the heavy luggage down.

"Wait!" he shouted and got his phone out of his pocket.

He talked quickly, nodded several times and everyone tried to get what it was all about from the small pieces of conversation they could hear.

"What's wrong?" asked Ignez.

"That was someone calling me back to say they had found Natalia's phone on the train to Garmisch-Partenkirchen and called me back, to tell me they had found the phone. Just without Natalia ..."

Not far from the group, the man who collected the bottles fell asleep.

The foyer of the inn looked typically Bavarian. Beautiful stags made out of wood, floral wreaths and embroidered curtains decorated a small group of chairs and a fireplace which hadn't been used in a long time. Just as planned, the group of actors arrived, but they all looked a bit unusual to the landlady. Those bright, colourful dresses, thick hair and a tall man looked almost like an invasion from another dimension.

"Do you want me to call the police?" she heard the man called Otto say. Apparently, he was worried about what had happened with Natalia's phone.

"Why? The police don't even try to investigate things like these. There are so many thefts these days. Sure, Natalia should be here by now, but she's not a child anymore. Bad news always comes faster than hoped for. I'm sure everything is just fine with her." Benta had always been the most reasonable in the group and was happy to take on the lead in difficult situations. The landlady nodded, but no one realised she took part in the conversation.

"Pavel said something could've happened," warned Otto, obviously concerned. The landlady decided to stay around for a bit longer. She cleaned up old magazines and eavesdropped in their direction.

"You know Pavel and it's a skill to take what he says seriously. I don't have this skill. Let's go to the parlour. Dinner will be served, and Bianca and Frederik are already coming down," mentioned Benta. Her dress had a floral pattern in blue and purple. It looked feminine and very impressive. She let everyone know that she was a woman who didn't have to hide. The landlady hurried before the group and opened the door to the parlour to show the way to those unusual guests.

"Did you all have a good trip?" Earl Rasnov came from the parlour out into the hallway to welcome everyone. His fancy clothes had their best days behind them already. The nice fabric didn't stretch much and covered up the skinny person under it. 'Charm is everything that ripens and remains, and even time didn't seem to spoil it,' thought Benta when she looked at him.

"Earl Rasno, you pedantic old impostor!" she greeted her old friend with a kiss. Benta thought she felt how an immature love between them both seemed to blossom.

"Please!" he said with a fake strict voice. "I'm not pedantic." He lifted his chin to act overly proud.

Everyone laughed as they all knew that he was the biggest impostor of all in this sector. The landlady laughed as well, as if she was part of the group, and showed Earl Rasnov to the door of the parlour.

"Benny prepared everything for our dinner, and I'll tell you about my new show. I hope everyone received their roles and proposals," said Earl Rasnov, and indicated the tables with an expansive, undulating movement of his arm.

Benny and Otto were already sitting there with their drinks and waved at everyone happily. They had a long and deep friendship.

Bianca looked paler than usual and stood close to Frederik.

"Your husband will behave despite all those beauties he could have here." Earl Rasnov separated the couple and sat Frederik at his side. Frederik and Earl Rasnov were good friends, however, since Elmira died, Frederik had secluded himself.

While a Korean woman dressed in a dirndl, a traditional German dress, took their drink orders, Earl Rasnov told everyone where to sit according to the place cards.

"Rasno! Why do we have to sit like this? It's worse than in school!" moaned Ignez. Shen needed a bit more space for all the ruffles on her dress. Big Creoles hung from her ears and her hair was darker than usual.

"Because what I have to say is important, and I don't want conversations interrupting my presentation." Earl Rasnov talked with his eyes half closed and his chin slightly raised, to emphasise his more important role in the group.

His voice sounded paternalistic enough not to get any contradictions. Once the waitress left the room, everyone was excited to hear about the new show.

Everyone was surprised when Benny got up and went to the front part of the room where Earl Rasnov sat at the left end of the table.

"I'm happy to see that everyone except Natalia made their way here today," started Benny calmly.

"Where is Natalia?" asked Virginia.

"Hopefully far, far away. Why is she still part of the group anyway, Rasno?" interrupted Ignez.

Benny looked for help to his father, who got up reluctantly.

"Please! We're professionals here. We don't have to love each other; we have to work together. And that's what it's about here. Natalia is a controversial person, but she had very good contacts and she's still Otto's wife," deflected Earl Rasnov.

"But not for long," said Pavel slightly snippily and put his hand onto his chest.

"That's not the topic now," said Otto.

"And when will it become the topic?" replied Pavel slightly impatiently.

"Please let us know, I'm very interested." Earl Rasnov sat down again, and Benny leaned onto the table behind him.

"I didn't want to address the topic in front of everyone else, but now, I think, we don't have to keep it a secret anymore. I'll leave Natalia. Please, I ask you all not to judge Natalia. I only married her because I didn't want to have an illegitimate child and to treat her like a slip … oh come on … I don't have to explain it, do I?" Otto felt slightly uncomfortable telling his story. He had to admit that he was naïve himself.

Fredrik became pale and put his hand in front of his mouth.

"You thought she was pregnant by you?" Benta was obviously surprised.

"Everything went out of control back then and she called me desperately, saying she was pregnant by me and I felt obligated to support her. We were good friends as well. I know that she can be a bit clumsy and I also heard about the problems Ignez had with the exhibition and Helene well … let's leave out the rest. I'll leave Natalia and will officially live with Pavel. I hope you'll all appreciate our relationship."

"Champagne, champagne. Oh dear. Finally! We all knew about our relationship, but it's amazing that it actually happened while I am still alive." Earl Rasnov got up and talked happily while he went to the door of the parlour and gave an order to the waitress.

The attentive waitress immediately understood and hurried to the kitchen.

"Does Natalia know her fate already?" asked Helene.

"No, we wanted to approach her. I found out about every lie towards Otto," emphasized Pavel.

"Please, Pav. It was an emergency lie. She's not a monster." Otto tried to calm him down.

"Ha, not a monster?! I doubt it!" Pavel acted as if he was spitting on the floor.

"Pavel, that's not how a fine … eeeh … husband behaves." Everyone laughed and the champagne arrived with the waitress and another waiter. The silver bucket had been polished until it shone, and every guest could see themselves in it.

"A toast to the couple! But could we go back to the initial topic?" Benny protested quietly. He knocked on the table three times, but he didn't get any attention.

Everyone toasted the couple and calmed down after a few mischievous comments about Natalia's fate.

"Please, silence now. Dad sent you all the scripts already and you can read up on your roles in there. We will present our show as usual, however, this time we'll be characters from horror films. The stage should look like a castle from Transylvania or something like that. I stated details for colour, sound and costumes on the second list which Helene will hand out. We have six days to prepare everything and the final rehearsal will be in Murnau."

Everyone looked at the lists and nodded. No one had ever been in the theatre in Murnau since the accident, and the memories of it were back immediately.

"What should we do if Natalia won't show up? She's not here. Did anyone hear from her?" Helene sounded pragmatic, as always.

"Oh, please, Helene. I'm sure she'll come and if I had to guess, I'd say she's confronted by every one of her business partners right now." Ignez railed against Natalia again because of the paintings she lost.

"Well. We'll wait until tomorrow and if she decides not to show up, we start looking for a substitute. The new actors for the 'bloody soirée' are young and probably interested in getting better roles. Otto, can you try to reach Natalia somehow?" Benny tried to calm the group down, but he didn't quite have as much experience as his father.

"I have to pick up Natalia's phone in Garmisch tomorrow. I'm waiting for her to call me back, but I can't reach her," apologised Otto.

"After breakfast we'll have the first rehearsal tomorrow. I hired new actors for the new show. Virginia, please take on Natalia's part until she's back and please train the new actors. Otto, let the police know that Natalia's not here and that someone found her phone. We don't know if something happened or not," commanded Earl Rasnov.

"We'll pay for food and drinks. Just please, don't drink any alcohol right after this delicious champagne," added Benny.

Just as Earl Rasnov asked, Otto called the police, who didn't really seem interested in a lost phone. Once he was back at the party, he tried to kiss his Pavel for the first time in public. Even if it wasn't as teasingly as in those romantic scenes, and not as skilled as a Spanish torero, as Benta said, he was still willing to make up for the lost time.

Everyone partied, was happy and no one was really interested in the absence of Natalia.

Further away from the noise and the party, the waitress and the landlady chatted about the two men kissing and how seldom something like this happened in a place like this.

✦

The scenery in Eschenlohe was wet even in summer and a breeze brought fresh air back into the valley. As soon as the sun found its way on the sky, the people of the town went outside for walks or to cycle. The first day the group was meeting, they had to be at breakfast at seven o'clock in the morning already. Earl Rasnov went with Benny door to door and asked everyone to get up.

Protests and boos came from different rooms. However, Earl Rasnov ignored them and determinedly went on to the next door. It was only Frederik who was dressed and was proud to be number two.

"Rasno, are we taking a taxi or the public transport to Murnau? Is there even a bus?" asked Frederik.

They had used the theatre for eight years. It was cheaper than the one in Munich and they could prepare better in it.

"We'll take the public transport. It only takes ten minutes from here and we don't have to find parking. It's hard to find parking at this time," interrupted Benny.

"Did you hear from Natalia?" Frederik asked, slightly worried.

"Don't know. Otto looks like he'd enjoy a bit of his new freedom with Otto. From my room at least, I could hear a lot of action from them last night." Benny pulled a face as if he were a hungry wolf. Frederik and Benny laughed because of the strict look Earl Rasnov gave them. He apparently wasn't a fan of the fun they both had.

"Dad," whined Benny.

A soft slap in his face indicated that Earl Rasnov still loved his naughty son.

In the hallway, Earl Rasnov shouted for everyone to come down to have breakfast. He was happy about all the screams of joy he got from the rooms and went downstairs happily. He wore the costume of a horror clown, which Helene had made for him. He wanted everyone to get in the mood for the new show already.

At the foot of the stairs the landlady was waiting, with a worried look on her face.

"Are we too early for breakfast?" asked Earl Rasnov.

The landlady seemed a bit confused by his choice of clothing. She rubbed her hands and Earl Rasnov immediately understood it as a sign of tension.

"There are a couple of men here and they wanted to talk to you and Mr Grossbeck." The woman didn't wait for the reply and didn't look at Frederik and Benny who came down the stairs behind Earl Rasnov.

"What's up, Dad?"

"Don't know. But I expect something bad. There are men who want to talk to me or Otto. I hope nothing happened to Natalia. I'll just get changed. The way I'm dressed now I won't make a good impression."

It took less than three minutes for the experienced artist to get changed. He approached his son and Frederik who stood there waiting. They went to the parlour where the breakfast buffet was prepared. There were two men standing waiting. They must have been in their mid-forties or early fifties. One of them wore a traditional Bavarian jacket and the other one the uniform of the railway police.

"Are you Mr Grossbeck?" asked the older one in the traditional jacket.

"No, I'm … Earl Rasnov, the head of the acting troupe. What's happened?" The short break before his name was hardly noticeable, but Benny thought how smart it was for his father to introduce himself to those officers with a pseudonym.

"I'm Inspector Vingard and I work in the region on the solution of homicides. The railway police told us they found a dead female body at the train station in Garmisch, whose identity we believe to be Natalia Grossbeck." Otto started to feel dizzy and Frederik's eyes lost their colour, as if they went glassy. Earl Rasnov was used to containing himself, even in difficult situation. He tried to calm his friends down.

"While checking the content of the body's bag, we found your address, as well as a note from last night, saying she'd be expected here. I have to ask Mr Grossbeck to come with us and identify the body." The tone of Inspector Vingard's voice indicated that he was used to his profession, but not as sensitive as they would have wished for at this moment. His traditional jacket was of a very good quality, but the dirt on it indicated that he lived alone and there was no one who helped him in the household. His hair was cut short, although his hairline was receding. He didn't seem overly excited by the look of the group in front of him, and Earl Rasnov was unfortunately very much used to the judgement of this region.

"Oh my God, Otto. I'm so sorry. Benny, please move all appointments and go with Otto and those men. I'll take care of the rest here." Earl Rasnov wanted to know more about what happened, but he thought it might be inappropriate at this time.

It was at this moment when Ignez and Virginia came down the stairs and interrupted their conversation to look at the strangers in the hallway. The inspector and his colleague stopped for a minute, intrigued by Ignez' beauty and the gentle and exotic appearance of Virginia. It would stay a secret what both men were thinking, but it was obvious by the look of their faces.

"Apparently, they found Natalia's dead body," said Otto with slightly shiny eyes. Something in his voice sounded like relief, but at the same time, he was rendered powerless by what had happened. Death is defined as the end, but for some who had already faced it, it was just the beginning of a new reality, which would forever have something missing. If it's an important or less significant person who exited from life, their loss highlights the mortality of ourselves. Everyone in the group faced it, especially Otto.

Ignez looked at the group and was obviously upset, thinking about what she should tell them and what not. Her skinny body moved between those men as if she was an unstoppable force.

"We'll go for breakfast. I'm sorry, Otto, but it saved us from having a lot of uncomfortable conversations." She took Virginia's hand and pulled her towards the parlour. She left behind a few people with dropped jaws. Hugo followed Virginia, wagging his tail behind her. The command for breakfast made him immune to anything else looking around him and he jumped over the feet of the men around him before he ran into the parlour where he sat down at the place where he had already sat yesterday.

Earl Rasnov looked at the inspector and his colleague and it looked as if he wanted to apologise for Ignez's behaviour, but the inspector was faster.

"Should we go?" invited Inspector Vingard. He was probably asking himself how people could show as little dismay after a case of death as these ones.

The reason

It was a completely uncommon encounter. Although tourists are welcome in this region, this group I met in Eschenlohe doesn't fit in here at all. It's mostly pensioners, lonely women, young families and sometimes even Asians travelling through Europe. However, actors, gays and impostors were challenging for me. Sure, I saw it on TV and the newspaper, but to meet them here was a new experience.

I looked at the back mirror of my car and at my own wrinkly face. I noticed that the husband followed me together with his boyfriend to the coroner in Garmisch. It wasn't morning anymore and my body was exhausted. I had been up since five a.m. and had to experience every type of weather there was already. If it was up to me, I would have left the motorway to go to the first restaurant to have a nap. But there was a strangled woman and a lot of open questions waiting for us today.

"Do you smoke?" asked the young colleague from the railway police next to me. It was obvious that he was nervous, and he was so inexperienced, it was almost refreshing. 'Good support for this investigation,' I thought.

"Not in my car." It wasn't like me to be very sensitive and I almost apologised for the way I said it, but I thought it might be better for my colleague to know from the beginning who the boss was. I don't smoke at all, but I didn't want to talk about my private life. I was just interested in keeping my car clean. Looking at my colleague's trousers, he was not a very clean person. I had to look at the collar of my white shirt guiltily and I didn't say anything else like it.

"I forgot your name again." I tried to distract him.

"Ralph," he said succinctly.

"What do you think about this group?" I was never very into theatre and art, except a few events with my ex-wife, which I would've rather avoided. For me, they were just a bunch of unemployed. I have to emphasise that I not only should have avoided meeting my ex-wife's friends, but also her. But those years belong to a past life.

"They really seemed to be hurt. However, I'm not a big help in situations like these. I barely have any experience. This is the first time in my life that I'll see a dead body." The boy was nervous and massaged his fingers. Judging by the colour of his index finger he wasn't a chain smoker; however, he was overwhelmed by this situation. A boy as young as him is mostly good for all the red tape and I hoped I could flee from the group of actors that way as well.

"Why did they ask you to help with this investigation?" I asked after I realised that he wasn't very chatty.

A lorry tried to overtake us and his engine went loud until it reached a dangerous pitch, which forced me to brake. I wanted to open the window to scream he should go back to driving school, but I was sure the driver wouldn't hear me anyway with all the noise. And even if he could, he probably wouldn't understand me. It was an Italian food transport lorry.

"I applied for the job. I wanted to get a bit more experienced jobs, but not really a homicide like this. I thought I'd work at the pass control, the customs, a theft or just something usual. After this appointment I'll stop working on this case anyway. I don't know what my boss thought when he said this was a case of theft."

I stopped him and hoped he wouldn't start crying. I'm not very good at comforting people and especially not men.

"The husband is a bit weird, don't you think?" I wanted to know if he also saw the husband giving his friend a kiss. I've never seen anyone as tall as his friend in my life. His tight trousers make him seem even more creepy and it looked like as if he'd burst out of them any minute.

'Brrr …'

I wanted to spend this time in the car with my own thoughts, but first my partner had to fight his shock and now he just shrugged after what I said. Apparently, he hadn't noticed anything.

We arrived at our destination and the computer voice of the sat nav confirmed it.

Once I got out of my car, I could feel the cold of the mountains in my bones and realised how tired I was again. The other three men got out of their car as well and the tall one comforted the widower. His big arms almost scared me, and his even bigger hands looked like those monsters of stone on cathedrals. As he kissed the husband again, I realized they were more than just friends. I didn't feel too uncomfortable. I know a lot of homosexuals who are here for their holidays. However, a man that big made me question my prejudices.

"You have to notify the guard over there that you're here. My colleague will bring you to the room where you then identify the dead body," I informed both of them and went to my colleague at the entrance for employees.

"The tall man over there is gay, isn't he?" I rubbed it in my colleague's nose to make him a bit chattier.

"Sure. I knew that from the beginning. Does this have any influence on the case here?" He sounded slightly too confident for me or he just wanted to show off.

"Where? How did you know?" I wanted to expose the know-it-all.

My colleague opened his eyes widely, as if he was shocked by my question.

"It was so obvious for me. Is it important for this case?"

I felt like an idiot as the boy seemed like he thought I was a great gossip and I decided not to say anything about it anymore.

"Hey? Is it important for us?" he insisted.

"I don't know, but if a woman dies, and the husband had an affair, I'd immediately look for reasons at the husband, but I think in this case it's something different." I finished my train of thought and wanted to avoid his warning look. Suddenly he became too self-confident for my liking and wanted to know everything better. However, I knew I had more experience and it was me who should lead this investigation.

"Nonsense. It's important to know if he loves his lover more than his dead wife or if his wife knew about their relationship. I was an actor for a few years and I know a lot about their ever-changing relationships. It could be she was only an alibi wife. That could happen as well." Oh dear! I didn't even think about anything like that, but the boy was right. But I still wanted to know if he just said it or if he really had a reasonable conclusion.

"What do you mean?"

"Some gays get married to a hetero just for show, and others because of the friendship to a woman. There are many reasons for a liaison like this. I think, the normal standards of society don't apply in this case." I didn't know how right he was back then, otherwise I'd have given the case over to my colleague. It really wasn't my case, but she was on holiday and I wanted some variety and took on this case.

The boy seemed to know more about this environment than me and he seemed like he recovered from the shock. He convinced me to have his support, as I knew that I had to overcome special obstacles while talking to this group. If Ralph was there, I could give him all the bad tasks.

"Do you think you could maybe help me with this case?"

I didn't want to admit that an acting group full of gays was too much for me, but in this moment, I thought it might be very helpful to have a younger person there who had different views for this investigation.

"I thought you'd never ask."

✦

Shortly after both cars with the officers from Garmisch and Otto, Pavel and Benny left the inn, silence came back to the place. However, the excitement of the news brought chaos with it which wouldn't calm down for a long time. Virginia slowly chewed her croissant and looked at Ignez with her eyes wide open. Once she realized that she didn't react to her looks, she tried to speak to her directly.

"I don't think you should have said all of this to the police officer." She quickly bit off another piece and looked down at the empty plate before her. Virginia wore her hair in a Norwegian bun to her right side. Her gentle appearance was in a big contrast to her character on stage. Nothing on her looked like violence or any kind of strong feelings, but her blue eyes hid an evil message which many would have loved to see.

Ignez wore an especially tight dress on this day and looked like she was a model right from the catwalk. Charming and distinctive, there were no other words for her look. She threw her long, curly hair behind her and slightly raised her eyebrows.

"As if you said anything better. I was just being honest. The police will find out about how much we disliked Natalia anyway. This horrible slut probably just got what she deserved. If it was me who saw her, I would've loved to hit her in the face several times. But I have to admit, it'd be too stressful for me to kill her." Ignez decided to eat a peach, thus proceeding with her breakfast.

"I'd have loved to push my throwing axe up her arse. She got Helene tangled up in some business and she won't tell me what it is. But it has to be more than just the stage in Berlin. For weeks, she tries to avoid me, talks on the phone from other rooms and now she even has some storage room and only she owns a key. I don't want to be a snitch, but she's no longer the Helene I once knew." Virginia waited for Helene, but apparently, she didn't want to come down for breakfast.

"Should we go out for a walk with Hugo? He looks so sad on his bench," said Ignez. As soon as Hugo heard his name, he made a sign to approve and to show that he'd be happy to go on a walk.

"He ate too much yesterday and he didn't like the long journey. I'll give him some camomile and fennel tea and he'll feel better soon. I'm sure they'll ask us about our relationships to Natalia. I'm scared no one will have to have a motive not to have hated her." Virginia gave a bit of ham to Hugo, but he just sniffed it, looked disgusted and turned around. Virginia poured some tea and cold water into his bowl and gave it to him to drink.

"Don't act like she is more important than she was. She was just a cheat. We missed all the hints and the death of Elmira is still on our minds. I don't know how I could prove it, but I'm so sure it was all Natalia's fault. As soon as we found out about all the problems she caused, no one liked her anymore. She caused trouble for all of us. Rasno only accepts her because she was a friend of Elmira. However, I'm sure if Elmira hadn't died, Natalia would have robbed her blind as well. There's nothing I'd put past her." Ignez stroked the poorly Hugo's ear.

"I hope Rasno won't change the date of our show. I need the money at the moment, and I can't use any of my talents in musicals." Virginia laughed as she imagined herself throwing knives in a musical.

"I don't drink alcohol, however, to celebrate I'd make an exception," said Ignez.

"I would drink so much rum and then piss on her grave and burn it." Both women laughed so loudly, Hugo got up immediately and joined in barking.

"Mother's coming. All three of us could go on a walk if it's okay for you."

There seemed to grow a certain kind of closure between both of them and Virginia enjoyed getting a bit more attention.

"Sure, I love your mother. Benta, come over to us," invited Virginia.

"*Buenas mi amores*!" said Benta. The aura of a prima donna was glowing around her. Her tidy hair and her purple clothes were matched perfectly.

"Did you hear the news already?" asked Ignez.

"Yes. Bianca just came over to me and told me that apparently, they found Natalia dead." Benta pulled a chair towards her and made the sign of the cross, like a good Catholic would do.

"We're about to take Hugo for a walk. Do you want to come with us after breakfast?" asked Virginia.

For the first time, Benta felt like Virginia would care about her and she asked herself what the reason for that could be. As far as she could remember, Virginia wasn't a singer and Benta never wanted anyone else on stage during her performances. Earl Rasnov was well aware of that. She decided to keep a close eye on Virginia.

"Sure. I'll just eat something. Did the police say anything? Was it a robbery? They found her phone, didn't they?" summarised Benta.

"We just met the police in the hallway, but Otto, Pavel and Benny all drove to Garmisch. Where are all the others? We're already finished, but Frederik, Bianca and Helene won't come down and Earl Rasnov drove to Murnau," said Ignez.

"Frederik's not well. Apparently, since the accident, he's not the same anymore and Bianca has to look after him. He's on medication. Frederik tripped over yesterday. Bianca complained because of what he said. He's not the lightest either. Helene, as far as I could hear, was on the phone. I just saw her right before she threw the door shut in front of me." Benta poured herself some coffee and she missed her Cortado very much once she smelled this brew in her mug.

Virginia looked at Ignez and found Benta just confirmed Helene's behaviour.

"Hugo's not too well. He doesn't like long train or car journeys," said Virginia.

"Come to me. You can have some bread." Benta started caring for Hugo, who seemed to feel better.

"Uhh, he never goes to anyone else." Virginia was impressed.

"So far, every dog loved me. Isn't that right, my dear?" Hugo replied with a slow wiggle of his tail and ate a piece of bread and butter which Benta gave him.

"I'm scared that even now that Natalia is dead, she'll still cause a lot of trouble for us," suspected Benta.

✦

Frederik couldn't eat anything for breakfast and went back into his room, right after the police left. The message about Natalia's unconfirmed death seemed to have hit him hard. He felt dizzy and he could hardly believe it when he went back into his room. He counted the rings on the curtains and continued to count the tops below them. His knee hurt a bit as he had fallen in the train the day before. Bianca helped him up but apparently hurt her hand because of how heavy he was. Since then, he repeatedly heard her moaning about it.

Again, red clouds appeared in front of his eyes and a slight sense of nausea seemed to push against his throat. Steps disturbed his concentration.

"What happened?" asked Bianca who was half-naked and not yet ready for breakfast. She smelled like myrrh, the scent of the cream for swelling. Frederik hoped she wouldn't repeat again how much weight he'd put on.

The farm décor of the room was the perfect stage for their drama. Frederik came from South Tirol where furniture had looked like this for centuries past. Bianca was from the Czech Republic where it was rural, fertile and wet as well. Everything seemed to be right and harmonic for both of them if it wasn't for the shine in Frederik's eyes which disturbed the panorama.

"I think they found Natalia dead in Garmisch." Frederik paused and went to the window. "The police were downstairs. Otto, Pavel and Benny went to identify the dead body in Garmisch."

Frederik's voice trembled slightly. The sun shone through the window and lit up his face. He looked even more pale and surreal than he had been when he entered the room.

Bianca finished drying her hair without saying anything. She watched her husband and thought about a way to calm him down.

"Everyone talks about it already. It was just obvious that eventually she'd cross a line. The little rogue did a lot of bad already and who knows what she would've done. Don't you feel well, my dear?" She threw her towel into the bathroom next door and got dressed while Frederik was looking for his timetable for the day. He knocked his middle finger on the windowsill and the voice in his head, which tortured him so often, came back.

'Ha, ha, ha. That hurt. Finally, someone had the guts to do what you couldn't. Poor fool. Tinga, tinga, tinga, tu.' Frederik's fingers knocked the rhythm of the dance on the windowsill and for the first time, it looked like there were the little legs of the demon in his head in front of him. He stopped knocking, rubbed his eyes and as he looked back on the windowsill, he saw his little, red and skinny legs dancing happily around. His first impulse was to check with Bianca to find out whether she could see and this demon as well, but apparently, she didn't notice anything of what was going on.

"Bianca, I think I don't feel well. Are you sure I took the right medication?" The fear in his voice was obvious, but Bianca was used to his anxiety attacks. She tried not to make them any worse.

"Darling. I'm not dressed yet and I'm sure you can manage for a little while, can't you? It's normal that someone dies. It's really nothing special in our age and it was just a question of time until it hit Natalia. Lie down for a minute and try to sleep." Bianca watched Frederik; whose look was focused rigidly on the windowsill.

"I can't continue to live like this," he gasped out.

"Fred. It's just one of your depressive thrusts. It'll be over soon." She went over to the cupboard where they stored their luggage and opened her small handbag. She looked for his medication and found what she was looking for. Frederik listened to Bianca pouring him a glass of water and the thought of what was about to happen made him shiver.

'Go on, lift your legs, lala, lala, I'm happy,' laughed the demon hysterically and tried to become a poet, but Fred didn't think it was funny at all. However, it reminded him that those legs performed the same dance as Elmira and Natalia did on the day of the accident.

"Here. Take this and try to get some rest in bed," ordered Bianca.

'The rope is falling,' whispered the demon.

Frederik offered some resistance, as if he'd want to see the dance of his small companion, but Bianca didn't leave any time for negotiations. He gave in and lay down again.

'Spot on!' laughed the demon, happy with himself, and he raised his legs.

Bianca looked through the window. In the entrance of the inn she could see Benta, Ignez and Virginia. Hugo ran around the three of them and challenged them to play with him. Virginia ran behind Hugo, who was a lot faster, and everyone laughed.

A quiet snore told her that the medication had worked, and she could leave Frederik alone for a while.

Once she reached the door of the room, she looked back into the dark room and at her sleeping husband. A tear rolled down on her cheek and she slightly bit her lip.

"Sleep well, darling. Sleep well."

✦

Hugo weighed only nine kilos and was quite small. However, his self-confidence was three times as big as himself. He was panting and walked through the open door to let everyone know that the three women would be there soon.

While he slobbered his water loudly out of his bowl at the entrance, Virginia and Ignez entered the inn. Ignez was first and looked relaxed. She seemed to be happy again, as if she never had the trouble with her exhibition. Her big earrings on her curly, black hair were a distinctive detail of her appearance. Virginia wore her hair in the hated bun, but this time she had decorated it with something blue she had found in one of the fields in the area. She wanted to emphasise her femininity with it.

The cold of the Alps was almost gone, and it had made way for weather which was almost Mediterranean. Several drops of sweat glowed on the foreheads of the women.

"Didn't you go out with Benta?" asked Bianca who had just come out of the parlour after finishing her breakfast. She was dressed plainly, and her wet hair was combed to the side. Bianca wasn't very much into gossip, but there was something weird about how happy she was. Ignez and Virginia, however, decided not to talk about it.

"Yes. She said she'd meet Rasno in Murnau where she wants to try her performance on stage. She took the regional tram about fifteen minutes ago. How's Frederik?" asked Virginia. She just had to notice how pale he was when they met earlier.

Bianca shrugged.

"I don't know. Sometimes he's better, sometimes he's worse and after such horrible news like that today, it just triggers his depression. I don't know what do to. I don't know how I can avoid someone taking him away from me one day because he'll need professional care. His illness seems just to get worse. Yesterday I had to help him stand and I hurt myself. I'll soon run out of strength. Ah! Before I forget, Mrs Meyer, the landlady, asked for you," said Bianca to Ignez who was caught in her thoughts, playing with Hugo.

"Me? Here?" Ignez was obviously surprised. "Are you driving off now or are you going for a walk?" she asked.

"I have to go to the post office and to the pharmacy and then I'll go to rehearsal as well. I can remember my whole show, I just have to clarify what it really was that Rasno wanted me to do. I think he can be too broad with what he writes, and I want to go over it with him today. What's your plan now?" She was now too curious, and she could have hit herself for it.

"I have to look where Helene is and then we'll go to Murnau as well. Why don't we go together?" asked Virginia.

"No, thanks. I'll see you all later." Bianca said goodbye.

"I'll go to Helene. I will be back in a minute. Will you wait for me? We could go to Murnau together." Sometimes Virginia sounded like a small girl without any hope, although she was well aware that no one could say no to her.

"Sure. Just let me find out what the landlady wants from me."

Hugo and Virginia went up the stairs, while Ignez was looking for the landlady. She sat in the front garden at the glass table and looked like she was busy with administration or some other tedious task. Ignez carefully came closer, but the smell of cloves gave her away.

"Hi. Bianca said you were looking for me?" Ignez had a bad feeling that something uncomfortable would happen to her now.

"You are … ah, right … one minute." The landlady finished another line in her book and nodded towards Ignez, indicating for her to follow her.

"I received this today by courier Apparently, someone knows that you're here and sent this letter here. I've never seen anything like this before. Whoever sent this could've waited for you to come back." She handed the big envelope over to Ignez. It looked like it was quite heavy.

Ignez opened the envelope and read the pages in it several times. The landlady didn't make an effort to cover up how curious she was and just waited in front of Ignez, trying to find out what this was all about.

"What?" screamed Ignez. She raised her hand with her elegant, long fingers to her chest and touched her décolletage gently.

"Is it something bad?" asked the landlady compassionately; however, it wasn't hard to see that she only wanted to find out more about what was happening.

"I can't believe it!" Ignez banged her hand against her forehead and made an unintelligible noise.

"Oh my God, what is it? I hope it's not as bad as it sounds." The landlady was so desperate for news, it looked like she was almost drooling like a hungry wolf.

"I can't explain it, but all of my pictures were found. [The thief wants me to pay him money as according to Natalia those are just copies. I worked for six months on this collection. I can't believe it!" cursed Ignez.

Full of rage, Ignez went up the stairs and her small heels almost hole-punched the wood of the stairs.

The landlady didn't understand everything but immediately got out her phone to call her fried. As soon as someone picked up, she didn't stop talking.

"Listen. Those actors who live here … Yes … Well, apparently, one of them was murdered and the other one stole some pictures. Imagine what kind of people live here. I'm so happy they paid in advance."

✦

'Oh God, oh God!' I thought.

In a country where everyone is used to different people, those men who sat in front of me were so different; they would attract a lot of attention. The husband had an average skin colour, his hair seemed to fade on some parts of his head, and he wore small glasses. He didn't look very intellectual and was not the type of man I'd imagined on stage. As he told me about his work, I thought about asking him if he knew any singers of traditional music, but I didn't dare. He was from Vienna and his accent and his loving eyes indicated that he was a charismatic man who probably had a very romantic effect on his audience. However, whenever a wife dies, most of the time the husband is the main suspect. My colleague from the railway police said goodbye to me. He needed to get authorisation for this consultation, and I was alone with those people.

The name of the second man was Benjamin Lutzow on his ID, but everyone called him Rasnov as it was the stage name his father used. I never understood what value artist names had, but I respected it. I could very well imagine that his father looked the exact same as him about twenty or thirty years ago. They both looked very much alike, despite their hair. Benny didn't seem to have much of it. He wore glasses as well, although his were more old-fashioned than the ones worn by Otto, the husband.

The third one was a mountain of man and I couldn't imagine how someone like him was actually gay. His passport told me that he was from the Ukraine. I don't want to buy into prejudices, but a body as big and hands as mighty I've only ever seen on films about gladiators. However, the kiss between him and his lover didn't leave any room for speculation about his sexual orientation. He was on the list of suspects as well, although if it was his hands around the victim's neck, they would have covered her whole face. I shivered, imagining something like this and I was slightly scared of this man. His head was as tall as a basketball and shaved completely. His spiky beard showed me that he was actually ginger.

"May I ask where you were yesterday? It's just for my orientation as right now, I don't know anyone in your group and if I understood correctly, you're all here because of a show, aren't you?" I started the conversation carefully and didn't want to step on anyone's feet. The Ukrainian guy started talking and I couldn't help jumping slightly.

"We were travelling here from Munich the whole day. Otto was with me the whole time." He put his elbow on the table and leaned slightly forward in my direction. I almost ran out of the room screaming. I managed to calm myself down by taking a deep breath.

"You don't need to be scared because of Pavel. He's more innocent than he looks," said the young Rasnov and laughed, while Pavel acted as if he was offended.

"Scared? Because of him? Come on. Why would I, right?" The small drops of sweat on my forehead contradicted what I just said.

"Exactly. I received a stupid text message from Natalia yesterday and we tried to call her the whole day, but she didn't answer her phone. Unfortunately, I didn't read it in time when she said that she'd be in Murnau at eight a.m. instead of six p.m. Please, don't get me wrong, I was married to her on paper but that's all. She was busy when God handed out the minds, if you know what I mean. So, whenever she said something stupid, no one listened to her anymore. I read her text message too late." It was hard for me to understand his dialect and I looked through the glass wall in the direction of the door of our office and hoped my colleague would come back soon.

"So she wasn't very intelligent. Do I understand you correctly?" I asked.

"She wasn't only stupid, it was dangerous how stupid she was," said the giant.

I just hoped he wouldn't bang his fist on the table. All the furniture in here was extremely cheap.

"Pavel, please. In her way, she tried to do smart things to earn her money. You'll soon realize the originality of what she came up with. She fell out with almost everyone in the group. Pavel has his reasons as well." Otto tried to calm his friend down.

"After the first examination of the body, my colleague suspects that she was already dead by nine a.m. That's why she didn't answer your call. Where were you at that time?" I asked even more carefully now, and I would have liked to hold the hand of the giant. If he were to lose it, he could cause a lot of damage.

"I tried on my costumes from six until he came out of the shower. Hmm …" Pavel broke off to think, and then continued. "Yes. He had a shower at about nine. That's when I realized that my waistcoat was torn, so I called Helene."

The lover had an alibi. The husband and the phone call. It didn't really calm me down and someone called Helene still had to confirm this phone call.

"What did the victim do for a living?"

"She was head of my father's dance school in Munich and mediated jobs to the group. We all paid marketing costs to her," interrupted Benny.

Despite someone having died, they all were too calm, and I started to think that they were all celebrating the death of this woman.

"A dance school? Does this really make any money?"

"I think so. I wasn't interested in her business for over a year. However, she had more money than me most of the time," said the husband in his simplicity.

At least, I thought, it was a possible hint. If she had more money than her husband, at least I could follow up on this suspicion.

My colleague from the railway police, whose name I still couldn't remember, came out of the lift and looked around until he saw us in the meeting room. He waved at me. I thought his behaviour wasn't right here. It looked like he was looking forward to this inspection. I nodded towards him and he came in our direction.

✦

The theatre felt even colder than the street Benta came from. Residual dampness was all over the room and even despite the radiator being on, it still wouldn't leave the room. Benta wore her winter jacket and a heavy purple suit with trousers and jacket made from thick wool underneath it. It looked like something women wore in the sixties. It was cold in Spain during the winter, and sometimes even colder than in Germany, but she could bear the cold close to the Alps. Her cold rosy cheeks were warmed by her woollen gloves, but they didn't make them warm enough.

"Rasno!" she shouted in the room. Her voice sounded echoey.

She came closer to the stage and stopped for a minute. She remembered the day when the accident happened. The insurance inspector lowered the stage halfway where the lamp hit Elmira's head. That's how it had stayed for the last two years.

"Here, Benta. I'm checking some things." Earl Rasnov wore his working clothes and looked like a character from the jump-and-run games. He stood on the left side of the stage at the switches for the stage.

"How do you feel – being back here?"

"It took a long time for me to be able to come back here. Did you know that Elmira's death was almost three years ago?" He sounded sad and caught in his thoughts. His eyes rested on a stick which could be attached to the decoration of the stage.

"It was an accident, Rasno. Eventually, we'll have to leave the past behind. You waited too long to continue the show. We will build it up all together." Benta and Earl Rasnov were very close and almost in love when they looked at each other. There was something in Benta's voice that made Earl Rasnov think what she had really said.

'Leave the past behind,' he thought. It was a hint that Benta was looking for a future for both of them, but he was still bonded to his wife, although he could barely remember her face.

"I still have nightmares about it. Benny as well. He doesn't talk about it, though." Earl Rasnov paused, got up and stretched as if he had just woken up. "Benny doesn't talk about anything. Sometimes it's hard to understand what's going on in his head," he said.

"Rasno, we're from another generation. When we talk to each other, our children twitter or text or whatever it's called. I'm glad whenever I don't have to use a phone. By the way, no one's called me on my new phone yet," said Benta in a mildly flirtatious fashion, took off her winter coat and threw it elegantly to the floor.

"Did you ever turn that thing on? I gave it to you so you could call me," he said, criticising her and indirectly told her how much he liked her. Benta closed her dark eyes slightly while she leaned her head gracefully to the side and put on a beguiling smile.

"I prefer writing and you can be happy that I turn on the computer to write a letter. I'd still prefer to write it by hand. What are you doing here?"

"I'm checking all corners and edges to make sure we won't have an accident again. The theatre has not been used for almost three years and although they cleaned away Elmira's blood, I can still see it there." Earl Rasnov pointed towards the floor where he had marked it.

"Unfortunately, she got hit in the middle of the stage, left of this lamp. Why did we even have those markings on the floor?" asked Benta.

"While Frederik was in the foreground of the stage to announce the dance of the dragonfly, the two dancers were supposed to step back in front of the background marking. The vines should have come down from the highest terrace for them to perform their part on the ropes. The ropes on this side got tangled on one of the lasers and hit my daughter on the head. The clamp wasn't attached properly, and it was my responsibility to check it. It had never happened to me before, but, well, I'm not as young as I was." Earl Rasnov moved to the spot where Frederik stood back then.

"Weird. We never talked about the details of the accident, but I was sure Natalia stood on the left side. The bitch always wanted to have her better side in the spotlight. As if someone like her even had a better side." Benta's reluctance towards Natalia had become worse over recent years. "Why was Elmira on the left side?" Benta went down the stairs in the middle of the stage to where the audience sat. She looked at the stage to get an overview. She had to step over some cables, and the remains of a broken speaker were in her way.

"That's what we realised on the first anniversary as well. When we met twelve months after Elmira died, Benny said that it really was an unlucky change to the plan. But despite me checking everything, it still is an accident."

"Who made this change?"

"Well, it was quite silly. Before the show, Natalia came to me. She was screaming and said that someone broke her wing on the left side. That's why she didn't want to go on stage on the right side. She desperately wanted to be the main act of the show and she and Elmira changed positions. It was a horrible mistake not to check it better." His face looked like it had collapsed because of this mistake. For the first time, he talked about the accident objectively and in detail.

"Rasno, Elmira was too submissive and if she had stuck with her place, it would've been Natalia who died. Did you never think about the chance that maybe Natalia tried to manipulate everything at the last minute? This bitch always manipulated us to get the main act on the show. To damage her own costume is something so typical for her. If it was me who she came to with an argument like this, I would have let her perform naked. She manipulated you." Benta's voice almost reached falsetto and the hatred of Natalia was very obvious.

"Well, I know that you hate Natalia, but back then I thought it'd be better to give in than to have one show less. Do you think Natalia's death has something to do with this accident? The thought kept me up all night. Benny said something like that as well and we wanted to approach Natalia directly, but that's impossible now." Earl Rasnov almost sounded too dramatic as he spoke down from the stage, but Benta could see some kind of sparkle in his eyes. He had a vision.

"We should definitely tell someone about this."

I started to get interested in this case when little Benny began telling his story. Apparently, he and his father had been busy investigating the death of his sister for over a year now. The insurance company classified the case as an accident and filed it away and the local police did the same. The investigator did nothing except put away the reports of the insurance company. There was no further enquiry. My new colleague from the railway police noted the information of the members of the acting group and got behind his computer. Again, I was alone with those three men in the conference room.

I felt like a cheap waitress of a motorway restaurant who served bad coffee. I gave them the old, chipped porcelain cups from our canteen and tried to get more out of those men after the surprising news from Benny.

"I was supposed to perform the dance of the dragonfly with two burning wings. The girls were to have taken them off in the middle of the stage and the dancers on the left side were to get onto the vines so that I could then spit a cloud of fire and they could dance around me." I was still slightly uncomfortable because of how big this fiery dancer was. While he explained his dance, he got up and at first I couldn't look past the big bulge in his trousers. I was so shocked, I decided to get more coffee before he lifted the other leg to perform another step.

Once everyone had fresh coffee and I calmed down, Benny continued his story.

"Well, later I noticed that as well. Normally, Natalia would've been the second dancer who was supposed to extinguish the burning wings backstage while my sister was dancing on a vine. However, back then, Natalia managed to convince my sister and my father to let her change role and position on stage. The police, as well as the insurance, both investigated the case, and no one had the idea that it might have been the wrong person who got hit by the light. Now that

Natalia died so tragically …" Benny paused and looked at Otto. I thought he probably didn't want to sound too cold. "It's just an assumption, but there could be some connection and I'm convinced it didn't just happen by accident."

I could follow him, and I had to admit that my colleagues should have looked into this a bit further. Something was "off" with the case of Elmira's death.

"My father said he just changed it because Natalia claimed her costume was damaged, and she didn't want to go on stage like this. Elmira agreed and they decided to change position on stage. I never suspected something to be off. It was nothing unusual for them to change roles." Benny knew more than that, but it looked like he couldn't remember just yet and I just looked at my colleague, who decided not to help me out.

"I couldn't go on that vine, that's obvious," added Pavel who imagined the show on stage. I was able to relate to what he said.

"Are the costumes still there?" I asked.

"Yes. It's Helene's job to look after the costumes, and I'm sure she didn't change anything on them, as the theatre was closed after the accident and our wardrobe has not been repaired." Benny stretched in his chair, and I realised I had interrogated these men for too long already.

"I'd like to take a look at the stage together with my colleague. Until now, I don't see any connection between these two events, but I don't want to exclude it either. Would that be possible?"

"Sure. Today we wanted to go over the new show. It'll be called 'The bloody soirée'. At the moment, my father has a rather morbid humour and he wants us to come back from the dead, as he likes to say. We will all perform as monsters to get a bigger audience for our show. It's one of Frederik's concepts." Benny paused and I realised that he wanted to continue, but the other two men stopped him. I noted it down to ask him again later.

"But there are hardly any people who want to go to a variety show in Murnau, are there?" I'd never seen a poster for a theatre in the region and I had been living there for a long time. However, maybe because of all the advertisements I just didn't realise it.

"Our theatre is in Munich. We just rehearse here, and we perform the first shows here just to test it. 'Must be Magic' was the former variety and should be on for six weeks in Munich. However, it was cancelled after the accident," explained Benny.

The door opened, and I barely managed to turn around.

"What does the theatre in Munich do? It must be quite expensive to have two theatres, mustn't it?" my colleague said, interrupting the conversation.

"The theatre in Munich is the dance school which Natalia was leading. All the costs are covered by ongoing contracts. We just have to pay for Murnau and it's quite affordable." Benny seemed to be the one who was responsible for everything related to finance.

"With your consent, I checked the finances of your wife," said my colleague.

When I realised I still couldn't remember his name, I discreetly tried to ask him again.

"Do you not want to introduce yourself? These men don't know you yet," I suggested and acted like I knew his name. I was sure he had told me, but I was too tired, I had been awake since five a.m. and I was busy with this case.

"Ralph Tschiplakov." Right, Ralph. I nodded as if I knew it all the time. Ralph neatly brushed his greying hair to the side and buttoned up his jacket. It was very professional, and I was slightly jealous. I looked quite pathetic with my chinos and the blue and white striped shirt I wore.

"Your wife was very efficient," he added, to my surprise.

✦

Finally, the radiator seemed to work again, and the knocking of the water pipes wasn't as loud as it had been a few hours ago. Earl Rasnov was scared that eventually the conduction would burst. Benta tried different positions on stage. Wherever she thought the acoustic was best, she marked the floor.

"The new spots can be controlled by a computer and they were really expensive. Can you tolerate these costs? We can't convince the audience with those old manual spots anymore. They're all used to the fancy spots from all those concerts," warned Benta.

"Benta and the other boys will bring the computers for the lighting and the cameras. The new stagehands will then assemble them." Earl Rasnov tried to go up the line again. Its engine made an even louder noise than the radiator and Benta jumped to the side to be safe.

"Rasno," she said thoughtfully.

"What's up?"

"But 'The bloody soirée' is almost the same as 'Must Be Magic'. I read through Frederik's script and I can hardly tell the difference. Well, we'll have different costumes and different make-up, but everyone will soon realise it's almost the same. We should try to improve the show a bit." Benta always checked everything carefully and never missed any detail.

"You're right. I especially have to say goodbye to the trauma I have from the last show. I checked every alignment and as Benny suspected, the clamp should have been fitted correctly. But it was secured to the wrong line. That's why the vine dropped on it. I don't think the insurance will give us more money now, but the police will have to explain to me why they didn't check it." Earl Rasnov was busy with his inspection and for the first time since the accident, he dared to stay on this high stage again. He wore his safety belt like a climber and banged with his gum hammer on every bond.

"Rasno! For God's sake! Come down, you wouldn't survive a fall from that high up. Come and help me with the acoustics. Helene should be here as well. Where is she?"

A loud click was followed by a hiss and Earl Rasnov lowered himself down like the pubescent boy he hadn't been for decades now.

"Ouch. I don't think that was good for my ankles," whined Earl Rasnov, who was aware that he shouldn't have done anything that exhausting at his age.

"Pull those ropes down so the others won't be reminded of the accident," warned Benta who saw that the ropes were in the same position as the vine which caused the accident back then.

"Helene is acting quite coldly. I don't know what's wrong with her. She said she'd be here, but she had to handle a few things beforehand. I thought she didn't know anyone here in Murnau. I suppose it has to do with something else then." Earl Rasnov massaged his ankle while he talked.

"Apparently, her relationship with Virginia is not what it once was. Ignez doesn't tell me anything, but Virginia and my daughter are quite close." Benta sounded very secretive and made fun of all the gossip. She looked at Earl Rasnov with great significance and laughed.

"You don't say. Oh no, oh no!" he shouted from the stage.

"What should we do without Helene in case she really leaves us now?" Suggested Benta.

Benta had stayed away from Earl Rasnov for one or two months, but everything felt very intimate and he had to wonder if it was time to start a future together.

"Someone will come up. The show will go on even after we're gone. We will also have to substitute Elmira and Natalia. I have some new applicants. Virginia was supposed to handle them," Earl Rasnov summarised.

At this moment, the front door of the theatre sprang open and a dog ran towards the stage and Benta, lightning-fast.

"Hugo, my dear! We haven't seen each other since this morning," Benta greeted the dog and kissed him a few times.

"What have you done so far?" asked Virginia. Her mighty hair was still in perfect shape and she placed her Norwegian bun elegantly on her shoulder. Next to Ignez, the other two just looked like two characters from a painting from the Renaissance.

"We looked for untied strings," explained Earl Rasnov.

"What's that supposed to mean?" asked Ignez.

"It means that we're not only here for the new show, but also for the last act of the last show," said Earl Rasnov significantly and leaned towards the audience.

✦

My colleague Ralph looked like he was starting to like this job. Initially he was a harmless and nervous chatterbox and now he was a valuable investigator. In little more than one hour, he had collected more important information on his computer than I had after my investigation. Everyone in the group of actors had transferred money to the victim; some of them had given her quite significant sums. I found out that Natalia advertised different artists and charged them for it.

I suspected that the victim was not killed for the sake of her phone. There could definitely be some kind of connection between her death and the death of her former colleague Elmira. I made it my task to find out what connection there could be. I just hoped that Ralph would stop disagreeing with me in front of other people.

"So, why did your wife receive money from every member of your acting group?" asked Ralph with his newly acquired confidence.

"I didn't know she received so much money. She advertised us and sent applications from the artists to other stage plays or agencies," said the husband.

"Of Ignez … her …" Ralph pointed towards a name on the paper. Apparently, he had difficulty pronouncing it.

"I can explain." The tall man called Pavel started to talk and I hoped he wouldn't get up to present his tight jeans again.

But Pavel got up and raised his big hands to explain what happened.

"Ignez is our stage designer and Natalia sometimes arranged exhibitions and other work for her. Natalia was known for having a lot of business connections. I have to admit that she wasn't the smartest, but she knew how to handle people to start doing business with them. Everyone has some kind of skill, and in her case, she tried to buy sympathy from the group by giving us good work. Ignez can tell you herself, but I'm sure that all the money she paid Natalia was for some work in Switzerland. Like commissions." Pavel stood next to Ralph, who sat on a chair. His crotch was too close to Ralph's shoulders, which irritated me a lot.

"Please sit down," I proposed.

"No problem, he should look at the other names here in my report," disagreed Ralph.

I was annoyed that he seemed to get along better with this group than I did.

"Who's that?" Ralph pointed to the paper and Pavel came closer and leaned over the report. I felt a slight tingle, but I didn't want him to ask me to be quiet again.

"That's Bianca. She can change each one of us into something completely different. She's responsible for a lot, including hair, make-up and backstage. She once changed me into a female singer with a massive wig …" I interrupted Pavel's unnecessary explanations and pinched my eyes.

"Yes, I can imagine, but in this case that's not important, I think," I said before he could continue his story.

"Why not?" disagreed Ralph again.

I was so annoyed, and I didn't know what to say so I snorted.

"Please. If you wish, go on." I felt excluded anyway and I had almost dropped everything to look after some other case. I wasn't prepared for my colleague to change that much. Apparently, he was better in handling the investigation on the computer as well. I would have needed a whole week for all of this. That probably was an advantage of working together with him, but admitting it took a toll on my nerves.

"She's in the hotel together with her husband. This afternoon, we'll all meet at the theatre in Murnau. Why don't you come with us and ask her yourself? She's a very open person and probably knows which work she got from Natalia." Pavel ignored me on purpose.

"Sure. Both of us would be happy to come," I lied. I was very jealous of Ralph, who seemed to get more popular with the group by the second.

"Ah. I think a group of special people like you is so interesting."

'Is Ralph trying to lick the boots of this group?' I asked myself.

"It's a date. We'll now go to the theatre. I'll call my father to let him know. My sister had already been dead for two years when my father had the idea of arranging a new show and presenting it as 'The bloody soirée'".

"How did your father get an idea like this? Was there a reason for it?" asked Ralph.

"As far as I remember, it was Natalia who suggested it," Benny said reluctantly. I was sure he was lying, but why?

✦

The unpleasant beating of his heart woke Frederik with an unfamiliar feeling. The medication Bianca had given him was strong and clouded his senses. However, he didn't know how long he could bear his problems without it. The dark room looked purple because of the afternoon sun, which was typical for this season in Upper Bavaria. The smell of his environment seemed like it was wiped out; Frederik couldn't even smell his sweaty body.

Frederik got a quick surge of emotion and after he calmed down again, he remembered that Natalia died in tragic circumstances. He wanted to get up, but his body wouldn't let him because of the effect the chemicals had on him.

He looked up at the ceiling and asked himself how he could survive this day. He was scared of his visions and wanted to make sure that those creepy voices, which tortured him so unexpectedly, wouldn't come back. He never talked about it with Bianca, but if they came back more often now, he felt like he would be forced to talk to her or someone else about it.

It was hard for him to get up and on the wet bedsheet the imprint of his body was still visible. He moved uncertainly towards the bath to wash off the unpleasant sweat. When he arrived at the door of the bathroom, he saw all those medications neatly lined up next to the mirror. He read through their names, but he had never heard of one of them. He didn't even recognise the letters and actually, he didn't even know if he read any of them.

He ended up just making peace with the thought that his doctor earned good money with whatever they were and that his wife should more know about them than himself.

He took off his wet clothes, let them fall to the floor and went to have a shower. A grey shimmer covered the room, and he was scared that it was the small demon coming back, but this time, something else happened.

When the water hit his greyish, thick hair, he felt a pleasant warmth running from his skin. Everything felt like it was happening in slow motion and he felt every millimetre where the water ran off his body. His erection confirmed that no matter what his state of health was, his libido was still the same. He enjoyed the increasing testosterone, and a hand grabbed his right hip gently and unexpectedly. The long and female fingers touched his erogenous zones which he had already forgotten about.

He couldn't open his eyes because he was still too tired from all his medications and right now, he just wanted to enjoy those hands touching him. He wanted to feel a goal for his animus. The smell of musk came through the water and into his nose which enjoyed the change of mood.

'Smell,' he wondered.

The woman's other hand found his left hip and her fingernails traced the way up to his genitals. The water became colder, which tempted him even more.

His eyes refused to see reality and he pushed his backside back to try to encourage the woman not to stop. The smell of musk seemed to mix with other smells and briefly, he thought about telling the landlady about those gasses.

When both hands found his penis, he moaned quietly because of a gentle bite into his neck. Teeth were traced by a seeking tongue which made him inhale sharply.

"Don't stop! That's what I needed," he said with a suffocating voice.

The water went colder and passed the point he enjoyed so much. His hand vainly tried to adjust the temperature, but he didn't want to stop what was going on just because of something like that. The fierce movements of both bodies were sensual and unusual for Bianca, who was normally more innocent. However, this change let him feel something he never felt before, something he had been searching for a long time.

Her teeth went deeper into his skin and what was lust turned into something slightly creepy. He tried to protest. The pleasing feeling became a horrible presentiment and her hands around his penis seemed to captivate his body. Her teeth came further up to his ears and at that moment he realised that it couldn't be Bianca.

His erection went as quickly as it came, and the water became ice cold. The cold pieced his skin like thousands of needles, and he forced his eyes open to turn around to the woman who held him.

"Come, darling. Don't stop. I want you. Don't you want me?" said a purple-coloured Bianca who was long dead.

Frederik whined and he wanted to break free from her hands, but they seem to hold on to him tightly. No matter how much he tried to escape, the arms of the abomination didn't let him go.

As he finally managed to scream, he realized that he was dreaming and that the bedsheet was wrapped around his body.

"Frederik!" protested Bianca. "Did you have a bad dream again?"

His beating heart had to calm down before he could answer her.

I went from the conference room to my car, without saying one word to Ralph. I let him feel what a bad mood I was in. He should realise that he was making a fool of himself, trying to take on the lead of the investigations and kissing the arses of this acting group. I thought it was a very childish behaviour and I definitely didn't want to let him do any of it. Unfortunately, I had already told my boss how great he was and how much he was helping me out in this investigation, otherwise, I would have thrown him out of my car on the next street corner.

"Did I do something wrong?" whispered Ralph innocently and with eyes as big as a rabbit.

"Let me drive. I can't talk while driving. How am I supposed to focus?" I replied thoughtlessly. Ralph looked to the side and ignored my anger. "I wouldn't mind you sharing a car with your new friends," I rumbled out of nowhere. Sometimes I lost control over what I was saying. Ralph turned red; apparently, I had finally found the weak spot I was looking for.

"My friends? They might all be suspects. Is this the way you want us to work together? You want me to share a car with potential murderers?" Ralph sounded quiet but superior. I was slightly embarrassed for the way I was acting, but I didn't care. He was the one who had acted unprofessionally, not me.

"Never mind. I'm driving. Be quiet!" I tried to shut him up.

"What's wrong? I thought we got along well until now. We wanted to investigate this together, and now you're feeble. Oh man, please, get a treatment." That hit home and he was right; I shouldn't have started it like this.

We continued driving for another fifteen minutes without saying one word and I wondered if I had put my colleague off now. I decided to act like he himself was to make him realise what it was that I didn't like about him. I also had to realise that I might have been jealous, but I refused to accept it.

"The giant walked around you and he almost stroked you with his crotch. I thought that was disgusting," I vented. His behaviour was annoying, and I thought it could also have an influence on the investigations.

"Don't be so childish. Just because he's gay and wore tight trousers you don't have to act like a virgin." Ralph waved his hand and ignored his colleague's homophobia.

"Don't be silly," I said, but Ralph didn't let me continue.

"Especially because he is the one who gave us the most information up to now. Considering that the victim was strangled and the size of his hands, I'd like to keep an eye on him. The other men are too small to do anything as physically demanding as this," added Ralph.

"I hadn't thought about it like that before. But he can't be the perpetrator. He has an alibi," I thought.

"His alibi is his lover. Please, even a rustic like you should know that a lover can be very jealous. Love is love, and if he decided to get a shortcut before they had an actual chance to get a divorce, he would've done it with his hands, wouldn't he?"

I had to admit that the boy had a better way of thinking like this group than I had. I just followed the facts, but Ralph seemed to have better knowledge about their background.

"Rustic?" I protested and tried to turn towards Murnau.

"Sorry, Inspector Vingard, but you will never get any information from this group. You look at them as if they came straight from their UFO. Your big eyes and the surprised look on your face is not the most favourable for us. I can see it, as well as them. And if I act a bit more sensitively around them, it's just because that's the best way to find out about the truth – as far as they know anything. If you keep asking them your way they'll stop co-operating soon." Ralph had won again and proved that he was the head of the investigation, which was embarrassing for me.

"If it was up to me, you can sleep with the giant to get the truth, but don't ask me for help." I was trying to be funny, but it failed miserably.

"Vingard!" warned Ralph. "You're a homophobe without any sense of humour and not objective at all. Maybe you should let someone else have the case if you're so disgusted by working with people like them."

I was quiet for a moment and had an impulse to apologise.

"Natalia, the victim, received money from every one of their group. Some gave her more, others less money, but everyone paid her. I read it in your evaluation. Still, she was almost broke. Did you realise that? I was immediately interested. And who knows more about Natalia's finances than her husband?"

I decided to stay quiet and tried to survive the roasting by acting proud.

"His lover. Otto seems like he's not interested at all in what his wife did. He barely knew that she had a bank account. It took a while until he had all the information because he didn't even know what bank it was with. And now we're going to the theatre and you're better off stepping back while I question all of them.

✦

Ignez was very interested in what Earl Rasnov had planned. She didn't fail to notice how her mother stepped affectionately next to him. She looked deeply into her eyes and made her understand that Ignez realised how much she tried to get Earl Rasnov's attention. Benta seemed slightly embarrassed and looked to the side. Ignez thought that her mother shouldn't have been embarrassed, but she understood and let her mother off.

"I'm so mad," announced Ignez.

"My *amor*. What happened?" asked Benta, slightly surprised and scared because her daughter could have said something against her newly found interested in Earl Rasnov.

"If Natalia wasn't dead already, I would've looked to kill her myself," said Ignez, raising both hands towards the sky. Hugo, who misunderstood, jumped up and danced around his tail and Virginia almost laughed.

"Not now, darling," ordered Virginia and wanted to laugh, but she thought that this was the wrong time.

Hugo decided to look for rats on the backstage, because there wasn't much for him to do in the little group here.

"They stole my paintings and now those thieves from Switzerland want me to pay them." Ignez stretched out her arms to show how desperate she was.

"Rasno, that woman was the biggest disappointment ever. I had so many problems because of her. She got Helene a contract in Berlin and since then everything has gone wrong. I never took one contract from her because I never trusted that woman. She was lucky in business, but unfortunately just her own purpose, but at least for this. This is something I really must admit." Virginia seemed to be venting as well, and Earl Rasnov tried to escape all the problems concerning Natalia.

"When I told Natalia she could lead the school in Munich, I just thought she could help our show with her business relationships. Until now, she caused more trouble than it was worth. That's what I wanted to say during this meeting. I wanted her to leave her job as leader of the school and then throw her out of the group, like Otto wanted me to," explained Earl Rasnov to calm the girls down.

"Are you serious? I didn't know about that. Why did you not just write a letter?" asked Benta.

There were noises coming from the foyer, but no one realised it.

"Well. I once called Natalia and talked about the problems Ignez had, because you told me about them," said Earl Rasnov, looking at Benta. "I realised that the business couldn't be as good anymore because of the few hours Virginia taught at the school, so I decided it was time to stop it, before the school became bankrupt."

"By the way, Natalia asked me to pay the commission of the courses in advance and up to this day, I still haven't received any money from any student and she never told me any dates. I assume she tricked me." Virginia picked Hugo up and sat him on her lap.

"That was a mistake. You shouldn't have given her money." Benta put on her coat while she was talking, as the room was becoming colder.

"Let me continue. Because of some questions Benny raised after investigating Elmira's death, I asked her to talk to me once she arrived here. Furthermore, I explained to her that we should talk about those finance issues we had. She surprised me by promising something she can no longer fulfil." Earl Rasnov paused for an unnecessarily long time.

"Continue!" asked Ignez harshly.

"She asked me to trust her and that she'd explain the accident to me. She said she could find out who was responsible for it. Back then, I didn't know what she was talking about, but I think she was scared. However, it could be that I just imagined it." The dark lightning of the theatre and the glow coming from the stage made Earl Rasnov's face look creepy. He had some special impact on the ladies by telling them all of this.

"Stop it, Rasno. She was a liar and extremely stupid. If I imagine that she wanted to blame someone else for something she did, it was just to get an advantage herself. Stupid people always manage to get by with tricks and fraud and Natalia wasn't any better." Benta's judgement was harsh but somehow justified.

They heard steps approaching them and two men entered the room together with the other members of the acting group.

"You are …" Ralph tried to guess.

"I'm Benta. How do you do?" she introduced herself, like she ever done to admirers, charmingly to the two officers. The smell of bergamot which surrounded Benta emphasised her charm.

"Benta. I really don't like to do this, but I have to disagree with that," said Ralph, equally as charmingly.

"What do you mean? Do you know something I don't?" Ignez' eyes looked like they were on fire because of her temper with the problem she was talking about before.

"I checked the finances of the victim and realised that she could not have been that stupid. She moved her money around quite frequently and if she thought she knew something; she couldn't have been sure what it was. However, if we all work together, we will find out what it was," explained Ralph.

Once it turned midday, the small clouds turned into a deep purple colour and the contour of the moon appeared on the sky. Helene was in a bad mood when she went over to the inn. There wasn't any sign of a smile on her face. As she entered the inn, Bianca and Frederik sat in the parlour drinking cups of coffee.

"Should you not be at the rehearsal already, Bianca?" asked Helene in surprise.

"Shouldn't you be there as well?" Bianca asked, also surprised.

"You should be at the rehearsal as well, right?" answered Helene.

"Right, but I feel like I am in some kind of predicament at the moment. Natalia put me in contact with this group in Berlin and they need a lot of my time, but they all seem to be quite successful." Helene's French accent was very obvious whenever she got excited.

"What does that mean?" asked Frederik.

Helene paused and apparently had to think about certain words in German.

"I should be here to do the stage together with Ignez and tomorrow and the day after I am supposed to be in Berlin, but I won't make it. Our stage is still in its trial phase and Ignez' plans aren't drawn in great detail, so I don't see how we will get it all done in time." Helene was exhausted and threw herself on a chair.

"That doesn't sound too good. It was a great effort for Rasno to get everyone here and it was certainly not cheap either. If you now go to Berlin, Rasno will be in trouble, won't he? What should we prepare without knowing where anything will be on stage?" Bianca was pretty nervous, and Helene thought that her news probably didn't calm her down either.

"I will somehow find a solution. Why are you here and not at the theatre?" Helene put her phone back into her pocket.

"Frederik doesn't feel too good after hearing about Natalia's death. It really is horrible. Even I can barely believe it. He had to lie down for a bit, but we'll leave soon. You can take the train with us." Bianca sounded as polite as always and obviously wanted to distract them from Frederik's pale face.

"Sounds good. I have to talk to Rasno about everything and maybe Ignez can decide the first draft of the stage. The plan for its moving and a tour or just small adjustments can be made after." Helene was very professional and well organised. "I think I was one of the only people who actually got along fine with Natalia. And that's what she took advantage of."

"Natalia? Not one of us liked this bitch. Who are those people from Berlin?" Bianca unambiguously made clear what she thought of Natalia.

"They have a show. More like a *Travestie Revue* where most of the audience are couples or businesspeople. It's a big theatre and very advanced, but they paid Natalia and she didn't transfer me the money before her death. She said that she wanted to bring the money with her, but now I haven't a clue. What am I supposed to do?" Helene would be even more devastated if she had known that there wasn't any money in Natalia's bank account.

"Did you tell Otto about it?" asked Frederik.

"I tried, but he doesn't want to know anything about Natalia's businesses in Berlin. And Virginia won't help me out." Helene got her phone out again and started texting.

"Talk to Rasno. He always knows what to do in situations like these and he is probably a pro when it comes to all the problems with Natalia. Are you going like this or will you put on something warmer before? It's freezing and if you catch a cold, no one will profit from you being there. Not here and not in Berlin either." Bianca won this fight and Helene got up.

"I'll be there in a minute. I'll just get a coat."

"We'll wait here at the door." Bianca pulled Frederik's arm which he yanked back in protest.

"My dear, it'll be a long time before I'm so weak again. I just took too much of the medication. Stop worrying now. Apparently, we have more problems with Natalia's death than we wanted. If Rasno finds out about Helene's contract, he'll explode like a rocket. We have to warn him gently. Without Helene, I'm sure our plans will fail." Fred had already recovered from his nightmare and tried to concentrate on his work.

"Fred. I'm more than sure that Natalia's death and all the fraud which will come up now will cause a lot of trouble in our group."

✦

The heating pipes made such a loud noise that Benta jumped and put a hand to her chest.

"I'll get a heart attack. Rasno, can't you do anything about it? This thing will explode," she complained.

"I don't think so, Benta. That's just air in the pipes. We ordered the caretaker to have a look and the workers will start renovating before the start of next month. It'll be good enough to rehearse. The shows in Munich will come later on, but everything seems to go as planned there," explained Otto.

"Well, Otto. I don't want to be overly fussy, but if what this officer … Ralph, is it?" asked Virginia politely.

Ralph nodded without saying anything and listened to their conversation.

 "Well, if what Ralph told us is true, we'll have another problem here. The money from the school is gone. Apparently, Natalia didn't leave any money in her account. Does she have another one, maybe?"

Otto decided to step in here.

"No, she doesn't. She had too much debt and I wouldn't have let her open up another account. I checked it today."

"Oh dear, Otto. Could you not have had a closer eye on what Natalia did?" Earl Rasnov was furious, as Natalia had always acted as if everything was okay. Now he was faced with finding out that a lot was about to collapse.

"I'm not responsible for what she did and actually I put the relationship behind myself. For the last twelve months, practically, I've just lived with Pavel." Vingard flinched and Ralph looked at him sternly.

"I can confirm it. Hours of doing the laundry, cooking and cleaning are my witness," whined Pavel and looked at his clean and manicured nails.

"Pavel, you're a drama queen. I can imagine Otto looking after the household himself," countered Ignez.

"If I may interrupt seeing as I'm the Inspector here …" said Inspector Vingard.

"Wait, Vingard. We're about to come to the point. But first I would like to know who else belongs to the group?" asked Ralph while Vingard turned pink and got up from his chair.

"Helene is my partner. She'll come together with Frederik and Bianca. They're still on the train. She sent me a text message," Virginia informed him.

"Frederik? Who's that?" Vingard interrupted.

"Frederik is part of the group and the cock of the roost. I think all women are fond of him. He can be difficult but he's fundamentally a nice man. You'll like him. He's our *maitre de ceremonie*. He sometimes introduces us and gets the audience for our shows, calling to join the show. He's also very funny," summarised Benta with a smile.

"Do women really like men like him?" asked Ralph and Vingard looked as if the question surprised him.

"I think he always respectfully stayed away from me and Helene. He doesn't have anything bad in mind, but sometimes he can be quite caustic." Virginia tried not to make Frederik's trait sound too bad.

"He's been my best friend since the beginning of the variety. Back then, my son and my daughter were children. I met him when my wife died," explained Earl Rasnov.

"Your wife died? What of?" Vingard seemed to be very interested.

"Nothing special. Just cancer." Earl Rasnov didn't want to start thinking about it now and he tried to change the topic by acting like it was nothing. However, Benta noticed how this question conjured up memories.

"Excuse the question. It was not very polite of me to ask," said Vingard. However, Earl Rasnov didn't notice.

"Leave it, it's your job." Earl Rasnov was obviously hit, and Ralph changed the topic.

"How was the relationship between Frederik and Natalia?"

"He can answer that himself. But I'm sure he wanted to have her as well," laughed Benny.

"Not in her current state. She put a lot of weight on," said Ignez and moved her long, skinny hands around her hips.

"She's dead, Ignez. We should respect the dead," said Benta to her daughter and told her to behave better.

"Inspector, I'm sorry, but Natalia didn't leave us many reasons to be sad about her death." Ignez was honest, but sometimes too direct. Inspector Vingard was increasingly concerned about her.

"But as far as I understood, there was something between Frederik and Natalia. Or did I not understand it correctly?" asked Ralph, looking for confirmation.

"Bianca will be happy to tell you all about it. The scandal was so big, no one could ignore it. But you should know one thing: Bianca knows about every one of Frederik's capers and she doesn't care. It was just funny. Nothing serious." explained Earl Rasnov and looked at Otto, who just stared at the floor.

✦

I knew that the good start with Ralph had now suffered because of my awkwardness and I wanted to make up for it. We left the acting group in Murnau because I couldn't take in any more information and

Ralph wanted to talk to his employer about our investigation. I was scared that he meant that I should look after my own problems and not to bother him anymore.

As I drove onto the motorway to Garmisch, Ralph still looked like we were both punishing each other with silence. I coughed twice but Ralph didn't respond.

"Have we fallen out?" I asked carefully. I was aware that he had found out about all my imperfections today. However, I thought this boy was quite nice. Maybe the fact that I was lonely since my wife had left me a few years ago had made me turn a bit weird. I wasn't used to being around people anymore.

"Nonsense. We don't know each other very well and I hadn't developed any personal feelings for you. I'm just thinking about this case." This was cheeky and he obviously wanted to sound dismissive.

"May I ask what you think about it?" A small cough made it very clear how embarrassed I was.

"This Natalia was somehow friends with the earlier victim. She wasn't very smart but good at business," summarised Ralph.

I nodded and went one lane further to the right as this conversation started to interest me.

"Yes. That's what I heard as well and also that this woman only delivered bad businesses. Apparently, she spent all the money of the other actors and from the theatre." An expensive car overtook us, and the driver looked obviously stressed. This led to me looking into my mirror and to checking my own face.

"The Spanish woman sounds more dangerous than she is. I think it's because of her temper, but still, I'll check this exhibition in Switzerland. It's crazy that someone steals her pictures and then claims that she has created plagiarisms. But this would mean registering it in Switzerland and lawyers there are very expensive. I suppose she'd rather pay the penalty to prevent a process than to fight it." Ralph stared into nothing and it looked like he'd draw the connections between the members of the acting group and Natalia, the victim.

"She will do, if she's smart. It's annoying but she was very naïve. The husband is still very far up on my list and his massive lover as well." I wanted to make some jokes about how tall Pavel was, but I was scared that Ralph wouldn't think it was very funny.

"Nonsense. Pavel is harmless. He's tall and impressive but not scary. The two women couldn't agree about Natalia, could they?" Finally, Ralph seemed to have forgotten about my misbehaviour and I tried to be co-operative.

"The lesbians?" It slipped out of my mouth.

"Vingard, please. I think it's not your place to label people because of such classifications. We want to investigate and it's important for us not to have a perspective full of prejudices. Please don't be mad but I think your prejudices are getting in the way." I thought to show my point of view could help the investigation to get more objective and I started to get angry as everything I said, the boy had something to preach to me about.

"The couple, I wanted to say. It's not that I have prejudices, but I only know people like them from the TV and … and …" Ralph interrupted me, exhaling the remaining air from his lungs.

"Well, the lesbians. Yes, I meant them. One got work from Natalia and will never see her money for the paintings. That'd be a reason to seek revenge, but only a weak one." Ralph was annoyed. It could also be because of the long day we had had.

"But to murder someone because of money is something that only happens in Mafia films. In the real world you'd sue someone until the money would be pressed out of their veins. Afterwards, this wouldn't be a reason to kill anyone as well. Do you want me to quickly stop at the restaurant on the motorway? I could do with a coffee," I said, trying to show a friendly version of myself, but I was sincerely burning inside.

"I thought about that as well and if I understood it correctly, is the … wait, who's the other one?"

"Virginia." I was better at remembering names than Ralph.

"Yes. It couldn't be her because Natalia didn't die with a knife in her back. Did you see how well she can aim a knife?" He almost sounded like a child excited about a circus show.

"Sure. We still have the stallion. The show master." Damn it, I'd done it again and judged someone too early. I kind of waited for Ralph to hit me, but fortunately he didn't.

"This man is traumatised, according to what Earl Rasnov said and what happened with all the women didn't seem to matter either. I'd say we should look for the reason why he has such a massive trauma. It's just an idea, but if the man really is in such a bad mental state, maybe we shouldn't put something like that past him." I parked in the space for visitors and was sure that I could score with my experience.

"We saw him for a minute when we were in Eschenlohe," I said to Ralph.

"True. He looked a bit shaky as far as I can remember."

"What happened here was planned. I don't think a man as shaky and traumatised as him could plan something like this. Let's go for a quick walk."

✦

The group was now together, and they all sat in the front row of the theatre and listened while Earl Rasnov introduced his idea for 'The bloody soirée'.

"I'm happy to see everyone except Natalia here." He looked at Otto and continued. "I didn't want to sound heartless, but I think in moments like these you never find the right words."

"I understand," mumbled Otto.

"It's okay, Rasno. I don't think anyone wanted her to be here. This woman did something bad to all of us. If I don't get my money now, I'll have to hitchhike to get to Berlin. Sorry, but Natalia was involved in more and if she treated others like that as well, I'm sure there'd be many wanting to kill her." Helene was far from being normal and sounded very hurt and bitter.

"We'll rehearse here for the next few days, even if not for the final rehearsal yet. I think many of you are still in shock because of this tragic accident. However, we have to keep living and move on. Virginia will instruct the new actors." Earl Rasnov's face was grey and he seemed small and resigned because of his new loss.

Benny got up, stood next to his father and skimmed through some scripts which he had brought with him.

"The reason why we met here is also something we don't want to talk about in front of the police."

The group started to become unsettled and they started chatting to each other. Two stagehands, who should have been looking after the new alignment of the lights on stage, dropped their tools for one minute.

"You there!" ordered Earl Rasnov with his full authority. "Don't stop!" They protested quietly but continued with their work.

Benny was convinced that the two men were busy with their work again and started again.

"We talked to Natalia about the dance school and our theatre at the same time and asked her to check the finances. We heard about what happened with Ignez, and Helene told us about the overdue advance money for her work in Berlin. I don't want to guess or blame anyone, but Natalia was in trouble. The younger investigator checked Natalia's finances and they were anything but in a good state," Benny told them.

Everyone looked at each other and no one dared to say anything. However, before Benny could continue, Benta started talking.

"Why did you not inform us on the phone earlier?"

Some supported her argument and others waited to see what would happen next.

Earl Rasnov turned in the direction of the stagehands who acted like they didn't see his warning look.

"Benta, it's already problematic that no one except Otto and Helene are able to talk to Natalia in a normal way. If I knew what problems it'd cause, I would not have let her stay in our group back then." Earl Rasnov coughed quickly and started talking.

"Well, we knew that if Natalia was in trouble, we had to be prepared that everyone here would be affected. We thought it'd be best to find a solution together. All of us invested in this theatre and Natalia started off being a good administrator together with my daughter Elmira. Apparently, this is not the case anymore."

"The police officer said that Natalia was broke and didn't have any money left in her account." Helene talked almost too quietly, and Bianca had trouble understanding her. There was a certain kind of sorrow in her face.

"Otto. Do you think you can get Natalia's bank details?" asked Virginia and tried to make eye contact with Helene. However, she seemed to have other problems on her mind.

"Now, I can, but as the police said already, there's nothing left." Otto was clueless and felt like he was partly responsible for what had happened as he had left Natalia alone and never thought about how she was.

"Why did you marry her anyway?" asked Ignez, who was confused by the situation. Her mighty presence was emphasised by her shiny eyes and Virginia especially seemed to notice it. Benta was happy about that.

"It was complicated back then. As many of you know already, I have been in love with Pavel for many years now, but I used to worry about this being just a phase. Natalia convinced me to have sex with her and it just didn't work. Later on, she came to me and told me she was pregnant. I didn't want to run away from my responsibilities, and Natalia told me she wouldn't interfere with my life, nor my relationship with Pavel." Otto didn't bother to get up, but everyone could understand him clearly and no one missed how embarrassed he was.

"One moment!" protested Pavel.

"Darling, not now. Everyone else is trampling on Natalia's dead body already," said Otto, but Pavel turned away from him and got up to show how angry he was. For two years, Pavel had had to be stuck in a role which he didn't like, and he didn't want to accept his fate.

"You should also mention that Natalia should've got an abortion. Otto offered her money, but she declined and said that she was a faithful person." Pavel laughed, thus showing his opinion very well. He raised his hand before Otto could interrupt him.

"This happened shortly after Elmira died and I get it that Otto must have been traumatised by what happened. That's why I decided to agree, but only until Natalia told us that she lost the child," Pavel continued vigorously.

"Oh my God, how horrible!" gasped Benta.

"Not at all, Benta. I did a lot of research and was really lucky to find out that this bitch had never been pregnant in the first place. I got the confirmation via email, right before we left. Her doctor said she was never pregnant. I asked for the invoices from the doctor and our office sent them to us. She just wanted to have a husband to look after her."

"Pavel, don't be so rude. Please, now you have to tell the whole story. Natalia was very depressive since the accident. I wasn't involved in her finances, but the fact that she gained more than twenty kilos came up in some conversations. She told me that it was down to the depression and the antidepressants. She had issues, just like anyone else of us. Please, don't be so egoistic. No matter what she did, we never cared about her problems as well." Otto was mildly irritated at Pavel's behaviour. He didn't like the sudden confrontation of private data of his dead wife.

"I didn't want to be rude," said Pavel so quietly that no one really understood him.

"I have to apologise as well. It was heartless from me to talk so badly about her for the whole time," agreed Ignez.

The others nodded and made incomprehensible mumblings.

"Otto. You should've said something as well. Maybe all the money she spent and especially our money, or all those unpaid invoices were part of her problem. That's the first I've heard about it." Earl Rasnov was surprised that Otto had never mentioned it before.

"She saw a psychotherapist, but I distanced myself from her and left her alone. I think I should've given her more attention, but to live with a manic person like her, it's not easy."

"No matter what, she'll always be a liar!" insisted Pavel.

"But that's part of her symptoms and we shouldn't talk about any of that." Benta asked Pavel for a bit more sympathy.

Benny paused and everyone looked at him.

"Dad and I are convinced that Natalia knew something about Elmira's death. She promised us to tell us everything here."

A tool fell from the alignment and Earl Rasnov warned them angrily.

"Damn it, out now! And don't come back till we've finished talking."

✦

Frederik and Bianca were back in her room at the inn and were sitting on the balcony. The evening wind blew cold air towards them and it made Bianca shiver.

"Everything Benny said today in the theatre was horrible. The boy wants to act like the investigator of this case now. Come on, he can hardly lead this group. Should we go inside again?" asked Frederik.

"Not yet. I'm speechless because of everything that happens here. Rasno really should've warned us earlier about all of it. Natalia really was dangerous." Bianca seemed to ignore the cold. Her mind was in another world.

Bianca and Frederik didn't hear someone else sitting down on their neighbouring balcony.

"I didn't want to shock the group with the other experiences I had with Natalia, but we should tell Rasno." Frederik picked up his teacup and took a sleeping pill.

The person on the other balcony came closer and eavesdropped on their conversation.

"That's what we'll have to do. It's true. I was always against Natalia being part of our group. Elmira insisted on it back then and in my opinion, Natalia only pretended to be Elmira's best friend. The only thing on her mind was her career and she didn't care about Elmira at all. Did you take your pills?"

Frederik nodded and pointed towards the empty box that had contained his daily dose.

"I'll talk to Rasno. You can't talk about this topic and I think you'd wreck more than you actually fix."

Bianca seemed determined to end the curse of Natalia's company.

Another slim woman stepped out on the balcony next to them and stopped after Benta raised her hand.

"I would've liked to do it myself, but I'm scared to have a breakdown if I talked about this topic."

"Fred, leave it. I know how to handle it and we've kept it a secret for too long already. We should've told him our concerns when we prepared the show of 'Must Be Magic'. It's partly his fault as well. That bitch was never supposed to get access to our group. She should've finished the season and then got work somewhere else. We have a lot of those supporting actors. You know it very well. We never needed to expand the main core of the group. Especially now that we found out that Otto left Natalia alone with all our investments for the theatre. He's a fool. He should've stayed with Pavel and just live his life as a homosexual." Bianca's hands pushed against the porcelain mug as if she wanted to break it.

'Tingle …,' Frederik could hear a voice from somewhere.

"Don't you think we should talk to my doctor? I think my medication might be too much or too strong for me. Did you say anything?" whined Frederik.

Bianca put her empty cup on the table and got up.

"No. Take your medication as the doctor told you to and lie down. I have to talk to Rasno."

Frederik did as he was told and went to bed. He felt increasingly bad. He felt like his senses were becoming sharper and smelled trouble. His heartbeat increased.

"I don't feel well. Maybe I should go for a walk."

"No, Frederik. It'd only get you more excited and you will just sit in front of the TV for the whole night. I'll wait until you fall asleep."

On the balcony next to them, Benta and Ignez still listened to their conversation and Benta raised her index finger to her lips to indicate that Ignez should remain silent.

"I wanted to look after Natalia as well, and now it seemed like she fell out with someone," explained Frederik thoughtfully.

"If this bitch hadn't faked her pregnancy, we wouldn't ever have noticed her existence." Bianca was making light of the situation.

"You should tell Rasno that as well. I'm scared that there's something that connects the death of Elmira and the one of Natalia." Frederik scratched his ear.

"Fred, you're hardly fit enough to remember the lines of your show. Don't stress yourself by thinking something like this. I'll go now before Rasno goes to bed."

Finally, Frederik did as he was told, lay down and Bianca tucked him in.

Bianca changed from being an appealing woman who did everything to make any libidinous dream of his come true, into a caring mother. The different roles this woman took on made her the most loving partner a man could ever wish for, thought Frederick, closing his eyes.

'Tra la la,' said the demon and Frederick couldn't face the full extent of his fear. His voice was frozen by his medication. His senses were alert and took in everything that was happening around him. He could hear Bianca leaving the bedroom.

"No," mumbled Frederik, already half asleep.

'Finally, we're alone, Freddy,' he heard. It was followed by a creepy laugh which announced the torture that was about to happen.

'Huhhhhm.' That was the only thing he could mumble before he fell into a deep sleep.

'You didn't want me.' A pair of legs danced before his closed eyes, but he saw it as if he were standing in front of the stage and the legs of his vicious demon moved up to the side.

'But now you're mine.'

✦

Benta shut the door to the balcony as quietly as possible and ran to her bedroom. She had heard Bianca walking away.

"I didn't want to listen to the conversation of others, and I felt embarrassed to make any noise when I came back in," apologised Benta.

"*Madre*, shame on you. A likely story. You just wanted to eavesdrop, and I bet you wanted to lean over the balcony to hear them even more clearly. Don't lie to me. What did you hear? Now I want to know it as well." Ignez had a hard time suppressing her laughing fit as she saw the embarrassed face of her mother.

"Frederik's changed a lot since what happened to Elmira. I think Natalia's accident was really hard on him as well. His eyes changed. Did you notice it as well?"

"Sure. Everyone saw it, but that's how it was last year as well when we all came together. As far as I know he's on quite heavy medication now. Bianca doesn't really like to talk about it. But according to what he just said, his medication must be more than just your usual sleeping pills. I'm ashamed because of how rude I was to Otto when we were talking about Natalia," said Ignez. "I think she was ill as well," she added, slightly concerned.

"Ah, it wasn't only me who had very big ears today. My goody-goody daughter likes to gossip! I don't care about Natalia, even if she really was ill. Otto should've warned us. Now that I know that it was her depression that made her put on so much weight, I finally have an excuse for my new body." Benta looked at herself in the mirror. Both women started laughing immediately.

"Natalia put on the same show about her being pregnant with Frederik. I don't understand why men have unprotected sex anymore. Something like this can happen to them all the time and they can hardly prove if it's true or not."

"That's true, but it needs someone who's not too bright as well and I think someone like Frederik is the perfect guy to pull something like this off." Benta wasn't very polite in the way she criticised Frederik.

"Well. She was cheeky. Sometimes, I thought we were friends."

"You are my daughter, but I protected you way too much. You're definitely too naïve." Benta took off her pyjamas and removed her hair clips.

"You're a heartless mother. I'm not naïve, I just believe in the good in people." Ignez defended herself with only weak arguments.

"I know that there's more Bianca wants to talk to Rasno about. I doubt that he can take on his role in the show because of the state that he is in at the moment. I don't want to think about what would happen if he collapsed during it. But we couldn't just take him off the show. We've been friends for so long and we're there for each other, even during the bad times. I have to admit that sometimes I'm sick of how arrogant Bianca can be, but we have to pay her respect for the situation she is in." Benta never thought of herself as the lover of Earl Rasnov, despite the unspoken love between them.

"*Madre*, what I heard earlier really blew me away. We should've really done something about this bitch earlier. If I imagine what it was that Frederik said! We all were in danger because of her. The operative word here is 'were'. Rest in peace, silly bitch!" Ignez spat out these words.

"*Hija*, she's dead and you have to respect the dead." Benta made the sign of the cross and put her hand on her chest to emphasise how outraged she was.

Ignez read an email on her phone and nodded a few times.

"Can you lend me some money?" she asked her mother.

"Why?" Requests for a loan didn't happen very often, but apparently Ignez had received unexpected news.

"Those Swiss people have made me a peace offering. If I pay them some money, they'll give me back my pictures and won't go to court. Benny said that in the event of them offering anything like this, I should take it, pay and finally end it. I think he's right and as I know that Natalia is no longer the head of our theatre and dance school in Munich, I have hopes that her successor won't cause as much trouble as her." Ignez looked her mother with an important face.

"Forget it. I just want to have a simple employment as a singing teacher, and that's it. One of your younger people can start doing that. Why don't you talk to Rasno? He could give you the job." Benta thought about that for a moment, looked at her daughter and smiled.

"What? Did you eat toothpaste?" joked Ignez.

"No, *mi hija*, but if I have to give you any money, it'll be under special conditions."

✦

Pavel stood in the bathroom naked and granted a look at his tainted skin. As he looked, worried, towards the mirror, Otto tried to calm him down.

"I'm getting old and because of your adventure with this bitch I had to spend the best years of our relationship as the other guy. I'm sorry that I just chatted away about her illness, but we had to explain why she'd put on so much weight. People would've talked about it if she were here as well." His voice sounded high pitched and Otto rolled his eyes towards the ceiling.

"Pavel, my dear. You haven't aged at all, but sometimes you're just evil. You've just got more mature and more distinguished. Sometimes you should really watch what you're saying. Please look in the mirror and tell me what you're actually seeing. You're gorgeous. Masculine. Strong." Pavel's chest seemed to grow bigger with every adjective.

"And with a horrible big belly. I got it while waiting for you to ditch your wife. I just stood on the balcony." Pavel's voice sounded mysterious as he said the last sentence and he stroked through his chest hair.

"Ah, you listened to the neighbours' conversations again. You should be ashamed," judged Otto. Pavel curtsied as a joke and waved his hand as if this judgment meant nothing to him.

"Nonsense. I didn't listen to anything. Frederik is so loud you can hardly not hear him and I'm sure everyone is worried about him anyway. It's completely normal to … well … be worried." Pavel checked his crotch and the beginning of his belly.

"Leave it and come to bed. I want to watch TV. Please, let's not talk about Natalia anymore. I will have to do enough of that with the police anyway," moaned Otto.

"Good, I agree. But I don't want to go to bed yet. I will have to start training tomorrow. I hope Rasno can lend me some money." Pavel wrapped a scarf around his neck and contemplated how much of his costume had to be changed to conceal the little belly he had.

"What did the neighbours talk about? Don't make such a secret out of it. You were out there for so long and without any clothes, I'm sure you'll have a cold tomorrow. Do you always have to run around naked?" Otto liked seeing his partner in his natural shape, but the cold was probably not the best condition to do something as daring.

"I hope to stimulate my blood circulation by being out in the cold. Did you know that Natalia tried the same trick with Frederik as she did with you?" Pavel seemed happy with the triangular scarf which he had created from his towel and he moved on to checking his hairline.

"I'd have to be at least ten degrees colder to stimulate your circulation. No, you're not losing your hair, love." Pavel looked at his moaning Otto warningly and continued with his treatment. "Which trick?" asked Otto, who was still so naïve.

Pavel put the towel back on its hanger and walked over to where Otto was lying in bed.

"She somehow told Frederik that she was pregnant from him as well," whispered Pavel.

"What?" screamed Otto.

"Be quiet. I don't want the others to hear us. What would Bianca think of me if she found out that I listened to them on the balcony?" Pavel tried to act innocently.

"Are you sure?"

Pavel raised his hand and put his other one over his heart.

"I swear. I almost fainted. But did you ever think about checking if it was true what she said before telling me you'd marry her?" It was more than just teasing from Pavel now and it hit Otto harshly.

"You're right. I always believed her. I'm sure her depressions were real as her pills needed to be prescribed. But let's leave the past behind us. Natalia is gone and I'm almost in a mood to celebrate. We'd have every reason to. We knew that Natalia wasn't pregnant." Otto tried to play the situation down.

"That's what I found out and I had to live with the consequences of this lie for almost two years."

"Could you excuse me, baby? Now I know why I love you so much." Otto tried hard to be charming.

"That's something else Bianca will tell Earl Rasnov."

"Are you worried?" asked Otto.

"Hmm. I just think we should maybe be the first to tell the police. I want to make sure we're not the suspects again."

"Don't be ridiculous. Why should we be suspects?"

"You're the husband and I'm the affair. Neither of us have a convincing alibi for when the crime happened," summarised Pavel.

"I never thought about this. We should give them the clinical record."

"I already thought about this. I'm the only one who could strangle her with my bare hands. Inspector Vingard keeps on looking at me weirdly."

"Maybe that's down to your … designer trousers." Otto smiled discreetly.

"My trousers?" asked Pavel insecurely.

Otto looked at his partner's hands, took them and started kissing them gently.

"Let's not talk about it. Your hands should look after something other than this brutal incident." Otto pushed his duvet aside and invited Pavel to forget about the sorrows of the day.

✦

Benta was already in bed and Ignez decided to go outside on the balcony again. She was still excited about her news from Switzerland and wanted to cool down in the cold. As she stepped out quietly, she saw Virginia, who cried and hid her face immediately.

Ignez looked around and wondered if Helene was close. She realized she wasn't.

"What's wrong, Virginia?" she asked without really hoping for her to reply. Hugo sat on Virginia's lap and wiggled his tail before he fell asleep again.

"I'm sorry, it's nothing," said Virginia and dried her tears with the back of her hand. Her beautiful wavy hair was all over the place and her normally larger than life appearance was almost invisible. She looked resigned and stressed.

"What's that supposed to mean? We're good friends, aren't we? Do you want to lie to me?" A woman as impressive as Ignez could look good even if she were clad in a dressing gown.

"I think I'm in the middle of a horrible relationship crisis. Helene's always so uptight and since what happened with Elmira, we don't get along very well anymore. We're just zombies which share an apartment. I want to live. I want a challenge and I hope the new show will help me out of my sad life and now …" Virginia couldn't continue and started crying again. Ignez hurried over to her and started comforting her.

"Please don't cry. Tears don't look good on you at all. You're strong, out of the ordinary and too sweet to let a crisis like this bring you down. Where's the old Virginia who turned Murnau upside down with me?" Ignez hinted at the walk they had taken together that midday together with Hugo.

Virginia tried to calm down, but she still felt too hopeless. However, she could get control before starting to cry again.

"A lot changed during the last two years and I have to admit not very much became better."

"Where's Helene?" asked Ignez.

"She's asleep. But we're just not getting along. The few good moments we share have become less frequent and I was stupid enough to push her into taking on the work in Berlin. It went so horribly; I can barely take it. She's blaming me." Virginia was obviously worried because of the consequences her recommendation had had.

"Natalia. Natalia. This woman messed up so much but it's not your fault. Natalia caused trouble for all of us and she was our agent in the end. I'd rather blame Rasno for being so naïve with his experience and not protecting us. But we have to move on and not worry about the mistakes that are in the past now but look for solutions and be happy." Ignez tried to motivate Virginia.

"Very smart," said Virginia.

"I'm sure I read it on some toilet somewhere." Ignez laughed about herself.

"What will you do about the problem with your pictures? Maybe I can recommend something else to Helene before she kills me."

"It won't be that bad. Helene is a grown woman and she should be responsible for her own decisions. I have a deal with those thieves, and I will get away with some harm. I'll ask Rasno to help me, and my mother wants me to take over the lead of the dance school in Munich." Ignez sat down in one of the rattan chairs and got out a red blanket to cover herself up.

Virginia summarised her situation. "Those people in Berlin won't accept a deal. If Helene doesn't deliver, she'd have to pay a fine and it'll be a big one. Even for two. She doesn't have enough money. Natalia didn't tell us about the downsides of the contract and our money for the material is gone now. Without material, there won't be a delivery."

Ignez didn't know a solution for her situation either and tried to cheer Ignez up by changing the topic.

"Did you hear that Natalia tried the same trick with her pregnancy with Frederik?" Ignez talked quietly and mysteriously.

"He really jumps into bed with everyone who has two legs. Oh man! I'm glad not to be one of them." Virginia felt better already and Ignez was happy to see her smile.

"When all of this with my pictures happened, I was so close to strangling Natalia myself. Although, I have to say, I'm sure I am not strong enough to break her neck." Ignez looked at her skinny arms, thought about how possible it was and shook her head.

"I saw the picture of the body. I thought that you really don't need any strength, as one of those trapeze ropes are enough," assumed Virginia.

A wind came quietly closer and became stronger and stronger.

"Right. But first you'd need one of them. Oh man! Should we go inside?" asked Ignez despite the blanket which was wrapped around her tightly.

"I'm afraid that I won't be able to sleep yet." said Virginia.

"We'll play cards, then."

✦

Earl Rasnov checked the dates of one of the bank statements from Natalia which Otto had downloaded for him. The aggravation was clearly visible on his face, as well as the past years which had been hard on him. Benny looked at his father and how he skimmed though those pages and was clueless how to help him. He decided to just sit on his bed and watch TV.

"Please turn down the volume. The others want to sleep, and we have to start rehearsing tomorrow." Earl Rasnov thought about how tomorrow would go and checked the account statement at the same time.

"Natalia really pulled our legs. Ill or not, she wasn't capable of working without being supervised," said Earl Rasnov.

"I don't understand why Frederik didn't tell us the story of Natalia's fake pregnancy earlier. Everyone knows about his stories with women and we won't forget the day when Bianca caught him together with

Natalia in the changing room. However, he should've told us that there was something wrong with Natalia." Benny talked slowly and tried to think about a possible connection to Elmira's death.

"I didn't tell Bianca we'd heard her story from three other people before. The neighbours really have an easy time listening to others on their balconies. That's why I booked a room further in the back for us. All the work one year after Elmira died was from old business partners which I know personally. People turn dodgier after something like this. I don't even know if these people here are ordinary businessmen, or some kind of thieves. We have to tell the police everything tomorrow. I don't want to get into more trouble because of this." Earl Rasnov threw his documents onto the side table and went to bed.

"We should be careful, as I don't want all the others to leave the group because of those troubles." Earl Rasnov realised this possibility for the first time and woke up immediately. He sat up straight in his bed.

"Did you hear anything like this from anywhere?" he asked.

"Not yet, but I have a feeling that there'll be a lot of change. The trouble around Natalia's death will bring a lot of other untold secrets out of the dark. Otto now living with Pavel …" That's where Earl Rasnov interrupted his son.

"Everyone except him knew that he was gay." Earl Rasnov laughed while he took off his socks.

"Dad, put it there where the dirty laundry is. Fredrik's juicy detail about his thing with Natalia …"

"That's no news either. Frederik would impregnate camels and elephants as well if we were part of a circus. I think we can forgive him."

"You and Benta are close to each other again …"

"Benny!" protested Earl Rasnov.

"Dad, leave it. Mother's been dead for so long, I can hardly remember her. It's time for you to look after someone else. I mean, I wouldn't move out of the house, but Benta would make a great partner and I like her too." Earl Rasnov was happy about Benny's judgement and he was thinking about this possibility.

"Well, your father is not the most handsome man anymore. I couldn't help but notice that I've deteriorated slightly." Rasnov massaged his feet.

"Dad, you don't have to beg for compliments. Smile prettily and take her out for some food, you can do that without me. We should look for a substitute for Natalia and maybe employ two new members. Our group is slightly over aged and we need younger and cleaner members who don't get us in trouble."

"You're right. I have to come up with something. Helene designed the costume for my horror clown, and I met one of her friends who is a seamstress in Munich. She told me that she'd be interested in the variety and even wrote an application."

Earl Rasnov was surprised and emphasised it by inclining his head slightly.

"Not a bad start. I told the younger inspector who was just here, that we're free for further questions during the coming days." Benny typed on his laptop and the ping of a sent email was heard.

"Please don't make us more work than we need. The police will call us themselves if they need something. I'm still so shocked about what happened, but I hope we'll find a good solution. The police will realise that Natalia became the victim of some drug smugglers. I hope no one has to deal with any of it."

"I hope you're right, Dad. However, I wouldn't bet on it."

Let's clean up the stage

In the early hours of the morning the cleaning team was busy looking after the seat cushions and the carpets. Earl Rasnov was watching them strictly so that no spot was left. Two electricians were busy attaching the new cables and installing the new computers. For a few years the lighting and the stage set had been made from elements controlled by computers. Earl Rasnov went from one to the other and instructed them, while checking their work.

"Something else is broken here," shouted one of the stagehands once he realised that the wheels of one of the moving stage elements didn't roll anymore.

"It's horrible. I should change all the elements, but it'd cost me a fortune," moaned Earl Rasnov.

"Dad, let these boys fix it and I'll try to get some resources from the state opera." Benny had very good connections to other theatres and tried to minimise the costs with his ideas.

"Mr Earl!" shouted one of the new members whose name Earl Rasnov could neither remember nor pronounce. Earl Rasnov just remembered him smelling of cheese.

"What's up?"

"We can start rehearsing," announced the cheese boy.

"Let's sit down in the fifth row. I want to see what Ignez' opening of the show looks like. She'll dance instead of Natalia." Earl Rasnov went on with steady steps, while Benny noted down which elements it was, he should look for.

Helene was slightly shaky today and she was looking for the right button on the computer. Once she finally found it, she pressed 'Start'.

The orchestra from the computer played now out of the speakers, as they hadn't ordered the musicians for the rehearsals. Despite the low quality of their speakers, the music was loud enough to be heard in the whole room. Benny wrote down some details concerning the technology and looked happily to his father.

Three spots were turned on and red light flooded the stage.

"Natalia wouldn't have managed that," commented Benny.

"I think she was a maniac. In case she put on so much weight because of her pills, she then was depressed because of that. What a horrible fate," thought Rasnov.

"Not as bad as murder," Benny considered.

A door of the technology room opened in the direction of the stage.

"We don't have a fog machine, Rasno. That's why you have to imagine the fog on the floor," shouted Virginia from the left side of the stage.

Earl Rasnov was a pro at imagining things, so he let his imagination free and fog came from both sides of the stage. The spots shone in a shade between purple and red, mixed with orange on the fog. In the centre of the stage, the curtains opened soundlessly and fire started at the same time from two spots. The magic of art filled the stage and caused a familiar feeling in the audience. A red light emphasised a masculine body which rose from the darkness. The giant wore a shiny blue waistcoat which was covered in sequins. The two fiery tassels in his hands flew through the air and painted a mighty vortex while the music grew to a fiery flamenco. Thunder came from the computer speakers and Earl Rasnov saved this sound mistake by hearing the music beautifully in his imagination. Pavel continued with his wild fiery game and Ignez danced around him. A vampire couple flew through the invisible fog while the bass became harder. On the side where Virginia stood were two stagehands pulling the flying stage into the back centre of the stage. The broken parts on it squeaked and Benny immediately noted it down. Virginia entered the flying stage, dressed in her costume. There were blunt knives attached to the stage. Quickly, seven knives flew towards a drum and as the last one reached its aim, Ignez finalised her dance in the centre of the stage and a cloud of fire flew above her head. The orchestra finished its performance with drumming and two notes from the harpsichords.

"Well done!" shouted Earl Rasnov.

Tears shot in his eyes and he got up to applaud.

"Well done!" he repeated.

Two splutters indicated the end of Pavel's performance and he approached Earl Rasnov while sweating from the heat from the fire.

"I think it's too dangerous for Ignez," he said in his soothing baritone voice.

"Don't be a coward. I want to see more fire. You can fart as well if you must," said Ignez loudly and Virginia screamed with laughter.

"The ladies have spoken." Earl Rasnov curtsied and applauded again. "That's the best opening I've ever seen. I don't want to change anything." His voice went away because of the hiccups he got as he was so excited.

"I'm just saying. I don't want to hear anything from her if she says her curly hair got shorter after it. Maybe I should wear more golden jewellery. I look too dark. More like a cursed djinn than a vampire. What do you say, Benny?" Pavel was never satisfied with his performance and even during the rehearsals he had to coquet.

"How was my idea with the wooden sticks?" asked Virginia.

"Quiet! Please, all be quiet! I have to sit down. You were all breath-taking," said Earl Rasnov. "Did you hurt your hand, Virginia?" he added.

"It happened while carrying the suitcases. Helene left me alone and I'm a bit clumsy with big luggage. But I'm sure the bandage will be gone by the time we start performing the show," she said apologetically.

"I just want to check the fire safety. We can't afford any mistakes with it. We're being inspected anyway, and the engineers will want to check it as well," warned Benny.

"How did you come up with this concept? I have to admit, when I saw it on paper, I couldn't imagine it very well. Fantastic! Again, I applaud you. You will steal my show." Earl Rasnov acted as if he was whining.

"Not at all. I bet you'll be unforgettable in your clown costume. I have to admit, I hated Natalia so much, I based this concept on it. I wrote it when I decided to seek revenge on Natalia." Ignez sounded proud and confident.

"We should be happy that someone else killed Natalia before, otherwise I'm sure she'd be the cruellest revenge seeker of all," verified Ralph who stepped out from the back part of the room.

✦

Ralph should already be at the theatre in Murnau and I'm happy that we agreed on sharing the work. I couldn't admit my own mistakes. It'd be hard to explain, and my boss didn't like me much as it was already. I parked in front of the holiday home and made sure to meet the husband on his own. Apparently, everyone was busy with rehearsing their show, so no one would disturb us.

His name was Otto and he sat on the balcony where he enjoyed the warmth of the sun. In this moment I thought my suspicion was confirmed. No loving husband could be this relaxed after such a brutal incident. It was this moment when I also remembered how lovingly the giant kissed him earlier. I shivered just imagining a mountain like this guy kissing me, or even coming closer to me. I stopped myself from thinking anything like this and went through the questions in my head again.

Only when I got out of my car, Otto realized I was there and waved almost too familiarly for my taste. However, I nodded towards him and locked my car with its electronic key.

"Mr Grossbeck."

"Inspector," replied Otto, who was in a good mood.

I sat down opposite him and spread out my documents.

"Thank you for taking time to answer my questions." I started the conversation diplomatically.

"Sure." He looked to the left and not into my face.

"You seem quite relaxed despite the fact that your wife died, aren't you?" Maybe I was too forceful, but he didn't seem to notice. He shrugged.

"I would've left her anyway. Despite her depressions, I was determined to live my own life and there wasn't any place for her in it. Do you know the story of my marriage?" Now he looked into my eyes and I realised that he felt relieved.

"Not quite. Tell me about it," I asked him and was increasingly interested.

"Natalia approached me two years ago and told me she was pregnant. We had sex once and I wasn't very careful. So I decided to take on the responsibility and that's why we got married." He paused.

"So far it sounds like the story of fifty per cent of men," I said, to try and encourage him to continue.

"Natalia knew that I was in love with Pavel and it was only because of the child that I agreed to marry her. We didn't make it a secret. Unfortunately, she became greedier and more possessive and eventually I couldn't live our life like this anymore. Today I know that she did have her troubles with being honest as well."

So far, I was really happy about how it had gone, and I wanted to get the handcuffs out to arrest his perverted giant. I nodded and just waited for him to continue talking.

"I know this type of woman very well," I said inadvertently. "Oh God, I'm sorry, I didn't mean to say it out loud."

"At one point I realised that Natalia's belly wasn't getting any bigger and I asked her why. She told me about an apparent abortion. Pavel and I tried to calm her down, but as we found out later by checking the doctor's invoices, she faked all of it. That's the advantage of private insurance. Unfortunately, I only received the email about her fraud on the day we left to come here. We wanted to talk to her about this. I could handle living with her for another while. Pavel took on the part as my lover and we couldn't live together. He was really angry because of it." Otto took a sip of his cold coffee which was in front of him.

"Like a mistress. I understand." I was sure that this was motive enough for both, to kill the wife.

Otto didn't think calling Pavel a mistress was funny at all. I wanted to seem calm and relaxed, but it looked like I had failed.

"Maybe you're right and I shouldn't have put Pavel in such a situation. It was quite egoistic of me. I didn't want my life with Pavel to become public news yet and today I see how stupid that was. Pavel did some research and found out that everything was just a show. Last week there was a massive confrontation between both of them, that's why he insisted on checking those old invoices. Meanwhile, I kind of moved out from home. For one year I've been living with Pavel for ninety per cent so far. As I realised the other issues from Ignez and Helene, I decided it was about time to come clean and get a divorce so I could finally live with the one I love."

"I understand. Do you mind me taking a look at your phone for a minute?" I lied, because I really didn't understand who the man in this relationship was. Maybe I should've let Ralph handle this. I didn't feel very comfortable admitting it, but I managed to keep my professional attitude.

"Earl Rasnov knew about what I wanted to do because of Natalia, and he agreed that we'd all say goodbye to Natalia here. It was only yesterday when I told everyone here about me and Pavel. Apparently, Natalia embezzled money from the dance school. Earl Rasnov suspected something like this already. To be polite, this woman was pure chaos. I suspect it was her mental issues that made her spent so much money on healers and other useless impostors. I don't know anything more about her and her death. Here is my phone," he finished happily.

I checked the list of text messages and saw that Otto really read the message of his wife yesterday.

"Did you know of your wife sending you a text on the day she died? Look, here." I handed the phone back to him.

"Right. She wanted to leave at six a.m. already, so she'd be in Eschenlohe at eight a.m. She was crazy, as so very often. We expected her at six p.m. I just quickly skimmed over it as I only heard from her when she was in trouble and I planned on talking to her about a very important topic. I really didn't think too much of it." Otto sounded honest and he shrugged. He didn't even seem to try to feel anything about the death of his wife, nor to fake any sympathy for it. I have to admit, I thought taking on the responsibility of caring for the child without being with its mother was something noble and I wouldn't have done it myself.

"So, you and your wife . . . ummmm … what should I say … did you …" I stuttered insecurely.

"If we had sex?"

I just nodded and tried to focus on my notes.

"I think three or four times. Not more. Natalia had other men. By the way, one of them was in this group – it was Frederik. I didn't care."

I was slightly overwhelmed by his point of view and I would have loved to have arrested them all for immorality.

"Is this important?" asked Otto.

I think I blushed when I said goodbye and went on my way to pick up Ralph.

✦

The air smelled of petrol and sweat. Even Benta's perfume couldn't cover up the pungent smells. Everyone looked at the young inspector in a very surprised way and thought about when he must have entered.

"Oh! I'm sorry. I thought it'd be fine for me to come on. Did Inspector Vingard not let you know that I'd be coming?" Everyone still looked at Ralph and no one dared to say what everyone was thinking.

"What are you doing here?" It was Earl Rasnov who finally said something.

"Well, I'm inspector in this case as my boss lent me to the detective squad," said the investigator apologetically.

Everyone nodded and barely moved. The young man felt increasingly insecure.

"I didn't listen to what you were talking about and I'd be happy for the situation not to become even more embarrassing. Please, call me just Ralph. Inspector is too formal." He blushed.

"Well, just Ralph, why are you here? Are we suspects or do you want us to be arrested?" asked Pavel challengingly.

Ralph squeaked like a mouse and laughed shyly, almost too shyly for an inspector. That's what everyone was thinking.

"Good joke. I have to remember that one. Would it be very unpleasant for you to talk about this case before Inspector Vingard picks me up?" offered Ralph, in a sympathetic way.

"Let's all sit down here in the front," ordered Benny.

The two stagehands opened the ventilation flaps and positioned themselves close to listen to the conversation.

"Thank you. While looking thought the data of the victim, I found a few details I have to talk about. Maybe everything will just turn out to be nothing at all, just like I expect it to be. Or maybe I'll actually manage to solve this case. Can someone explain to me how the financial arrangement between Natalia and the group was? There seems to be a lot of trouble, and I want to know what's going on." Ralph got back his composure and talked a bit more confidently.

"We have this theatre here, which was closed since the accident. We paid the rent, but we didn't have any shows in here since my daughter died. However, my father didn't want to give up this investment. My sister was leading the dance school in Munich and if we had a show, we started the season there. We could hold one hundred guests there. The stage is not very big, but definitely enough for our show. After Elmira died, Natalia took over the dance school and started as our agent," explained Benny.

"It was only the act with the fire which we couldn't perform there as well as here. The ceiling is too low," added Pavel.

"That's not important," said Virginia.

"What was it that Natalia did in Munich?" Ralph asked.

The two stagehands moved the ladder a bit more to the front and listened more.

"Natalia worked as a dance teacher and as our agent, like my sister did as well. Natalia really helped us out during the first few months and did a lot for us. Everyone tried to support her as much as possible, as we were all dependent on her work as an agent. Unfortunately, she gained a lot of weight and it wasn't as easy for her to dance as it was before. That's what we had to consider. I just heard of it, but I think it answers some questions I had before." Benny was very focused on being as detailed as possible and Ralph gave him a signal to tell him that he understood but he didn't dare to add another word.

Everyone listened and Ralph wrote down some details from the story.

"Until six months ago, maybe eight. Something changed and Natalia started to refuse to pay and payments in advance, as well as regular payments just seem like they all went wrong," added Benny.

"That's when I got a job at an exhibition in Switzerland and my pictures got stolen. I ended up with a massive loss because of Natalia. I think she had already lost control over her finances," interjected Ignez.

"Helene didn't receive her advance payment for her work in Berlin either," said Virginia. Everyone nodded.

"The rent for the school in Munich is due as well. We wanted to get rid of Natalia from the theatre and the dance school. She promised me to deliver something I was looking for a long time. That's what she said. I didn't want to put her off on the phone already because I wanted to know what she had to say, but I guess I won't find out now," added Earl Rasnov.

"Sorry, but I want to highlight something in particular," stated Benny. "I checked the alignment where the lamp was secured, and I was sure that someone had manipulated it." Everyone looked at Benny with an interested look on their faces.

"An accident like this one doesn't just happen out of nowhere and I didn't think this was an accident anyway," he continued.

"What did you think it was?" asked Ralph impatiently.

"Natalia swapped her place with my sister on the day of the accident. If she hadn't, it'd be Natalia who's dead now and not my sister. Do you understand?" asked Benny and waited for Ralph to agree.

"My God, why didn't you tell us?" asked Benta, who was obviously shocked.

"Because this could prove that it was Natalia who caused the death of Elmira."

The air between them was loaded and everyone felt the adrenaline in their veins. One of the stagehands held his hand to his chest and his jaw dropped.

Almost everyone was talking about the suspicions and hints from Benny. But only almost everyone. Helene seemed to be slightly withdrawn and grappling with her own problems. No one noticed her leaving the theatre by the back door.

"Where are the others …? Wait …" Ralph consulted his notes. "Yes, here. Frederik, Bianca and Helene. Will they not be here today?" he asked.

"Frederik's not very healthy these days and the long journey made it even worse. We hoped for him to recover and rehearse with us. However, it looks like as if he won't come. Bianca looks after him, but we expect them to be here in the next hour. That's what she promised us on the phone. Where's Helene? She was here a minute ago," wondered Earl Rasnov.

"I have to ask a few more questions. Apparently, everyone in the group has a good alibi and I only have a few open things on my list here. Benny, why did the insurance company stop investigating this case? Did they not believe in your suspicions?" Since first meeting them, Ralph had grown more involved with the acting group and he sounded very friendly while talking to them. What started off as being a formal conversation was now a chat between friends.

"Benny, back to your suspicion. Please, I don't want to start any conspiracy theories, I just want to understand why they stopped working on this case after your sister died." Ralph had turned out to be a good investigator and everyone felt comfortable talking to him so far.

"I noticed we record our shows. We do it so my father can check the shows, correct the lighting or change the course of the show," started Benny.

"Is there a recording from the day when the accident happened?" asked Ignez.

"No. Unfortunately not. No one turned on the recording, but that is something that can happen. Frederik might've been at the box office and I was probably busy with something else. No one had time to handle the technology, so no one did it. But there were a few more things that happened on this day which I remembered after the investigation. Natalia was on the wrong side of the stage. She talked to my father about something which I didn't understand afterwards." Everyone listened to Benny and Ralph wrote down everything he needed. They all seemed to be uncomfortable by thinking about what this all meant.

"But Natalia wanted to hide a flaw in her costume on this day. I can remember it clearly," said Helene, who just came back to the group.

"Which flaw?" Benny's glasses were reflecting and hid his green eyes completely.

"She ripped something off it while getting dressed and she didn't have time to check it. So she changed position with Elmira. That's how I remember it. Sorry, I didn't want to interrupt so much." Helene wasn't sure if this information was needed.

"Did you not tell this story before?" Earl Rasnov's eyes changed slightly and he was obviously interested in what she said.

"Everyone ripped their costume somewhere. I don't do anything other than fixing costumes in this group," said Helene snippily.

"Please. Next time I'll fix my waistcoat myself. What a victim you are!" snorted Pavel.

"You're a victim yourself," disagreed Helene confusedly.

"Both of you, shut up!" interrupted Earl Rasnov. He indicated to his son to continue telling his story. Pavel pulled a face at Helene and he looked like the Ukrainian version of a mad Frenchman. No one noticed it and Helene raised her chin in the other direction. Their fight because of the damaged waistcoat was something that had been going on for a long time now.

"But the costume wasn't ripped at all. I saw it myself. When you told me on the phone, I went to the wardrobe and checked it. There wasn't anything torn." Benny spread his hands and showed how clueless he was.

"That's weird. I didn't fix it either," said Helene thoughtfully.

"You don't say! You didn't fix that one either?" mumbled Pavel. Helene was annoyed and got up.

"I can't do this anymore. Before we all witness another death, I'd rather go for a walk. Someone has to fix the damned waistcoat of this giant baby." Helene's steps were so firm, they were very loud even on the thick carpet.

"You're really stupid, Pav. Leave her alone." Virginia tried to defend Helene.

"She doesn't do anything anymore, am I the only one who realises this?" Pavel wanted to get up to continue moaning, but Earl Rasnov showed his full authority.

"Sit down!" Pavel did as he was told immediately.

"Well, Natalia didn't stand on the spot where Elmira should've been. She was almost thirty centimetres off. I realized it because of my notes. The spot wasn't on her properly."

"Natalia was so stupid; she couldn't tell the difference between left and right. She only stood on the right positions on stage by accident. Sorry, but this doesn't prove anything." Benta just listened to Benny so far and tried to follow his thoughts.

"Still, when I mentioned these facts to her, I also told her that my father wanted to talk to her about the finances of the dance school. She just said that once we heard what she had to tell, we wouldn't care about any of this anymore. She said she wanted to reveal a secret of some fact about Elmira's death. We were curious about what she had to tell." That's how Benny ended his story.

"I think the fact that Natalia wanted to tell you about the death of Elmira or declare an old case as a murder, could've been a reason for someone to stop her from coming here." Ralph was desperate to hear more, but Elmira's death seemed to be more of an accident than murder and he wasn't sure if it was worth investigating anymore.

However, everyone realised that both deaths could be linked. The two stagehands had moved the same light up and down for almost an hour and looked at Earl Rasnov, whose face looked creepy and angry in the shadow of the lighting.

Let's fix the costumes

When I arrived in Murnau, I looked for a parking space. Tourists from China or Japan had arrived in the city. They walked around like ants and their groups blocked the small streets. I was already annoyed and wanted to go home. That's when I saw Ralph, who was waving at me. It wasn't his best trait. He didn't look very masculine when he was waving at me, however, I decided not to mention it to him.

"Hello, Vingard." Judging by his broad smile, his conversations with this group had gone better than the questioning of the husband.

"The husband can hardly be the perpetrator. He didn't like his wife, but their marriage was over anyway. She wouldn't have been a problem for him and his giant partner. What did you find out? Please tell me everything." I asked him this drily and straightforwardly. Working with Ralph was interesting, but I wanted to make sure he knew that it was I who led the case and I was only interested in a professional relationship.

"I can see that we have to investigate Elmira's death as more than an accident." Ralph started the conversation in a very moderate voice followed by a summary which didn't come to an end and almost lasted as long as the way to Garmisch.

"Come on," I interrupted him. "You were there for barely two hours and you talk so much, I started thinking how many days it'll take me to write the report. Did you check the alignment?"

"I'm not a forensic scientist, nor a technician. Why would I check it? I'd only see a heap of metal and nothing else."

"And why were you there? You should've called me immediately. I'll send the forensic scientists immediately tomorrow."

"Vingard, don't rush it so much. After two years now, I don't see just one chance for us to find another hint there. I think I did a good job with my part of the investigations. Sure, if you didn't have so many prejudices, you would've had a better questioning. That might be true, but I got us a lot of information."

He was right, and I was mad about an investigator with so little experience getting so much good information, while I just had a conversation with the husband which led to nothing.

"Those mad people didn't mention one word about investigating by themselves. You should know this really could be a motive for the death of our victim. It would be crazy to think what happened if this old man finds out who killed his daughter. We can't be certain that it is murder yet, but this man seems quite creepy to me."

Ralph should have called me immediately. He listened to me and I tried to combine his thoughts, but I still didn't know enough about the accident on stage.

"We're in the beginning of our investigations and I made appointments with everyone in the group. I told them that they should attend those appointments on their own and everyone seemed to co-operate. No one acted suspiciously. Or, let's say, most of them. Hmmm? I just thought of something."

Mr Know-it-all remembered something, but I had to cut back on my protests as a bus tried to overtake me. I snorted loudly and signalled to him to continue talking.

"Helene, the one who does all the costumes, seemed a bit off and there's a dispute between her and Pavel. I don't know why this would be important, but it didn't fit in the harmonious picture of the group. Benny told him about the suspicion that it was supposed to be Natalia who died on the stage when the lamp came down, but she swapped position on this day. And the recording device wasn't turned on. Quite strong indications that there's more to see, right?"

It wasn't likely at all that the giant man was the perpetrator according to the husband. Moreover, if I remembered correctly, he could've cracked open the whole head of the victim with his bare hands. Just like a nut.

"I received an email. The victim was strangled with a belt or a leather strap which she had tied around her bag herself. Everyone was sure about that. I would have liked to get pictures from the train station in Munich, but my colleague informed me that it'd be about four weeks until the material was analysed. Apparently, the success rate was very low as we don't know who we have to look for." It was very disappointing, but I acted like it was a success and hoped for Ralph not to minimise what I found out.

We had almost reached my office. I still had to organise the meeting rooms and I knew that the woman who was the office manager would be mad at me again for not letting them know earlier. She always caused trouble. Suddenly, I remembered a joke.

"Do you know Ms Hiersemann, the woman who is in charge of the organisation?" Ralph looked like he was still lost in his thoughts.

"No, not really. I think I saw her once. Why?"

"Let's split our tasks. I'll write the report by using your information and you'll help her organise the appointments for tomorrow. Would this be okay with you?" I could cuff myself, but I decided to make this beautiful boy suffer a bit.

"Sure, no problem."

'That's what you think,' I thought.

✦

The room in the inn smelled like fresh varnish and oak. Frederik was still lying on the bed and seemed slightly dizzy from the sleeping pills. Bianca was watching TV when there was a knock on the door.

"How's Frederik?" asked Earl Rasnov, who had come back with the others.

"He's still a bit sleepy but he'll get up in a minute. I'm sorry, Rasno, but if he doesn't feel any better soon, we'll have to cancel our part of the show. What happened and the journey stressed him too much and I have to admit, it stressed me as well." Bianca seemed upset and her eyes showed that she had cried earlier. Earl Rasnov was used to the feeling of watching a partner collapsing in front of him and he knew that it was impossible to forget about.

"Are you okay, Bianca?" asked Benta sympathetically from behind Earl Rasnov.

Bianca nodded silently and opened the door slightly. Her hair was slightly all over the place and her clothes were sweaty and wrinkly.

"We all have to go to Garmisch tomorrow. I talked to the investigator and he told me that we all have to be there. You have to think about if Frederik can make it. Benny told the police about our concern because of Elmira's death. Benny has this idea, but I have to admit, it now makes sense to me." The friendship between Frederik and Earl Rasnov was quite old and he didn't want to leave his friend hanging during dark hours like these.

"The other investigator was here today. Vin … something, the skinny one. But he didn't ask anything important. He seemed to be more interested in Otto's and Pavel's alibi than in what I had to tell him. I told him about my shopping in the pedestrian zone, about the pharmacy and about Frederik. He barely noticed it. I felt like I was just an old woman no one was interested in." Bianca actually looked disappointed. She smoothed her hair and tried to rearrange her clothing.

"Bianca, my dear, not noticing you would be a mistake no one would ever make. Let Frederik get some rest and go downstairs to see the others. I'll check on him. He looks as if he'll wake up soon anyway. I did this back then as well. It'll do me some good. Leave us men alone," recommended Earl Rasnov and pushed himself into the room. Benta thought his behaviour was quite harsh. She pulled down her lips and showed her disagreement.

"What do they want in Garmisch? Every investigator should know by now that no one will miss Natalia. They questioned us about what we did on the day of her death as well. I hate officers. They'll steal the whole day from us." Bianca snorted and went in the parlour with Benta while Earl Rasnov sat down next to his friend.

Fredrik was asleep for a few more minutes, but as soon as Earl Rasnov sat down in the chair, Frederik started mumbling.

"What's up, Fred?" asked Earl Rasnov.

"Medication," whispered Frederik. He sounded tired.

"Do you want me to get your medication?"

Frederik shook his head and signalled to Earl Rasnov to help him. He got up from his chair and reached out for Frederik's hand.

"No. I can't take those horrible pills anymore. They make me even sleepier than the ones before. I want to go." Earl Rasnov pulled his friend up and pushed the duvet aside. Back in the day, Frederik's legs used to be nicely tanned and his veins looked nice and strong under his skin. However, now they looked a bit weak and his underpants hung from his waist like an old cloth. Rasnov became sad and he would have liked to hug his friend to comfort him.

Frederik's eyes stared into space while his feet were looking for the ground to stand on.

'Me left, you right.'

"Shit, no!" screamed Frederik.

"What's wrong? I'm just helping you."

'Pregnant ladies with hiccups lose their children. Glup, glup, glup. Ha, ha, ha.'

"I have to take a shower." Frederik shook his head heavily.

"I can help you."

Slowly they went into the bathroom and Earl Rasnov sat on the closed toilet seat, while Frederik tried to manage standing under the shower.

Frederik's posture relaxed once he turned on the water.

"Rasno, we have to talk about a fake pregnancy," said Frederik while the water ran down his head, his body and his feet.

✦

The inn normally didn't have as many guests and most tourists tried to avoid staying too close to the centre of Eschenlohe. It was a common fact that the priest didn't care too much. He ran the bells every hour and every fifteen minutes, even during the night. For years, tourists tried to complain without being successful.

The landlady changed all the windows and put up heavy curtains which almost completely blocked out the noises of the crazy priest. Sometimes guests from other holiday homes came into her parlour and she tried everything possible to distract them from the noise of the bells. During this night, she played traditional German music at a moderate volume. She tried to cheer her sad guests up slightly.

"What will you do now?" asked Bianca.

"We'll cancel my apartments and move to Pavel's. I'll send all of Natalia's stuff to her mother. I don't want to keep any of it. The time with her was nice, but I'm glad it's over now." Otto seemed relieved more than worried. Apparently, he was over his initial shock and seemed hopeful for a happy future.

"This farmer from Garmisch looked at us as if we were from the circus. He didn't understand the difference between a variety and a circus group. It's sad that people like them know so little about people like us." Bianca drank her tomato soup and her lipstick lost a bit of its colour.

"He didn't seem to like me nor Pav. However, I realized something which made the conversation slightly more interesting. Natalia thought she needed to be here in Eschenlohe at eight. Apparently, she opened her invitation the wrong way and must've ripped off the number one by accident. The inspector can hardly understand the way our world works. Whenever he talks to us, he jumps up and down in his chair. I can't stand it. That's more than old fashioned. As if we'd even be interested in such a dry old mummy as him." Otto was still upset about the conversation with the inspector. Pavel came back from his talk with Benta and interrupted him.

"Oh please! Men like him, all uptight and dressed in old trousers from the seventies are the dream of every lonely heart. I won't comment on his hair. I can already imagine the conversation we'll have with him tomorrow. You can see me starting yawning already." Pavel acted as if he had to start yawning.

"After what Benny said, we should all be careful. We were all there when Elmira died. Should it turn out that there's a reason for another investigation, we might have to quit our theatre until it's over. It's a nightmare," explained Otto.

"But only one of us was there when Natalia died." Earl Rasnov came in together with Frederik and listened to the end of the conversation.

"We all had enough motives to hate her, but it seems a bit melodramatic to wish her dead. I suppose she had some dodgy meetings with all those thieves she was hanging around and opened her mouth a bit too wide. In the end it must've caused an argument." Helene's anger towards Natalia was obvious.

"At least she was one of us. We should have a funeral service as well. It could happen that every one of us will spit on her coffin, but we should pay respect to the dead." Benta tried to lighten the mood.

"I don't like thinking about this investigator who probably suspects one of us of murder." Virginia looked at everyone testingly and thought about the possibility of it.

"The problem is not him thinking it was one of us, but two. Or maybe that a murderer from us killed two women. It really is horrible. Let's eat and think of something different.

"What about thinking of 'The bloody soirée' for a while?" Everyone applauded Ignez' proposal.

✦

Pain in his temporal lobes forced Frederik to close his eyes and to touch his forehead. The pain was like a rusty caterpillar which slowly moved along his parting towards the back and made him shiver.

"Are you having hallucinations again?" asked Earl Rasnov quietly with his hand in front of his mouth.

"I don't know. Could you please take me upstairs? I don't want to upset Bianca anymore," said Frederik. Small drops of sweat on his cheeks indicated that his body had reacted and asked him for relaxation.

Earl Rasnov cleaned Frederik's lips with a cloth napkin as they were coated in icing from the cake he had before. He got up discreetly.

"Where are you going, Dad?" asked Benny.

When everyone looked at him, he knew that there was no discretion anymore and he lost his posture slightly.

"Look at this. This happens when children take on the lead. Now I have to sign off every time I decide to get up. Benny, your father isn't senile yet and doesn't wear nappies. Leave it. I want to talk to my friend. I'll be back shortly." Earl Rasnov and Frederik were slightly confused when they left the room and did everything they could not to attract more attention. Frederik quickly talked to Bianca and happily said goodbye to everyone. They went upstairs and as soon as they entered the bedroom, Frederik threw himself on the chair and inhaled deeply.

"I have to talk to my doctor. When I read that hallucinations are a possibility, I didn't expect anything of what's happening to me at the moment. I almost have cramps in my head. I want to work on this show, but it won't work if I'm on these pills all the time."

While Frederik was talking, Earl Rasnov gave him some water.

"Here, drink. Maybe you haven't been drinking enough or something simple like that. What's bothering you? What kind of hallucinations do you have?"

"In lighter moments, once the pills wear off slightly, I see a lot of which I think is true. But once I take the pills, I feel foggy. The doctor said to me that it's normal and not hallucinations but daydreams. But never mind. I don't feel well anymore." His beautiful eyes and those well-shaped eyebrows reminded Earl Rasnov of those earlier days when they met and went from bars to discos.

"When you said that we should talk, what was the reason behind it?"

"Natalia."

"I know, but why?" Earl Rasnov sat down on the chair opposite him and looked at his friend.

"Not important anymore. She's no longer with us and we have to focus on the future. I won't be able to be part of the new show. Maybe I'll work in the background, but I can't risk anything on stage. If Pavel or Virginia perform the dangerous parts and I mess it up, it could be that we'd have to close down. So we should accept it as it is now, and I'll leave the show now. At least I'm still walking on two legs." Frederik looked tired and defeated. The unflattering yellow light in the room made him look almost grey and for a moment, Earl Rasnov thought about how he could pull through with his show without his best friend.

"Who could be a substitute for you? It'd definitely not be me. Natalia was in the end, despite all the problems, the reason for us to fight against one problem all together. I made her part of the group on purpose. I wanted to create some kind of balance. Sometimes a common enemy is very useful. Now Helene seems to have her own plans and you want to leave the show as well. I still don't have anyone to take the place of my daughter. Man, I see myself standing in front of a pile of debris," said Earl Rasnov resignedly.

"Rasno, don't be so pessimistic. Eventually, we'll all leave the show. I think it's time for Benny to take on my role. He's twenty years younger …"

Earl Rasnov interrupted him softly. "Thirty-three years. That's half of an eternity."

"That's true. We should help the new generation and not stand in the way of it. I can feel there's something up with Helene as well," noted Frederik.

"Natalia handed her work from Berlin and took all the money herself. Helene asked me for an advance payment, but as far as I understand her situation, a simple advance payment won't be enough. Those are very dodgy people and I warned Natalia about them. However, every time someone said no to Natalia, she did the complete opposite." Earl Rasnov was worried and gazed through the window [in the room].

"I'll talk to Benny tomorrow and let him take over my role. I can help you with the direction. Would that be good?" asked Frederik.

"Yes. I'm afraid someone is here to see us. The younger investigator who was in Murnau just parked his car. You stay here and get some rest. We'll see each other tomorrow."

Earl Rasnov went quietly and closed the door behind him. Frederik got undressed and checked every corner of the room before he went to bed. He turned off the light and the numbers on his digital clock shone in the darkness. Even the moon was gone, and the stars didn't come out during the night. The dark cloud which he could see took shape and seemed to turn faster and faster. Frederik closed his eyes and tried to relax.

'Wake up, darling. We have to make love,' said the demon feistily.

✦

Loud laughter came from the small parlour of the inn. Ralph was slightly insecure when he entered and smiled at the group. However, something unexpected happened. They all stopped laughing and talking immediately and looked curiously at Ralph.

"Sorry, I didn't want to interrupt." They seemed tense and watched Ralph eagerly. "Good evening," he added. Some nodded, but still no one talked to him. "Virginia invited me," Ralph said apologetically.

"I'm sorry, where are my manners? Please, come in." Earl Rasnov appeared behind Ralph. It made him jump slightly.

"That's right, Ralph. Thank you for coming."

"I was a bit unsure in the beginning, however I couldn't let the opportunity pass of hanging out with famous actors of the local theatre outside of work." Ralph sat next to Pavel who looked at him sceptically.

"Is your colleague here as well?" asked Pavel. The indication between those lines was too obvious.

"No, we're alone," Ralph said flirtatiously. Pavel screamed loudly and took Ignez' hands.

"What? Alone? It almost sounds perverted." Pavel laughed and the mood in the room became more relaxed.

"It's not pleasant to have Mr Vingard staring at us like animals in the zoo. I spent almost two hours with him this afternoon. He's not very … cosmopolitan, is he?" said Otto.

"I don't want to talk badly about my colleague, but I have to admit that he can be a bit rough every now and then. But we don't want to talk about this, do we? I promised Virginia to turn up here outside of work, without any investigation." Ralph turned out to be a very chatty man, especially for someone who worked in investigations. They all ordered something from the waitress who positioned herself behind Ralph. Even he ordered something.

"I invited him so he could get to know us better personally. He said it could help him with his investigations, but he isn't here to interview us," explained Virginia.

"Yes, right. There'll be a lot of work tomorrow. That's why I just wanted to ask you something about your theatre. I was part of an acting group back in the day and I did training for two years. However, one day I decided to go into the police force and here I'm now. I've been working as an investigator for two years now, but this is the first time for me to do something this big." Ralph looked around to see who was here.

The waitress looked happy when she came with their drinks and she turned up the music. Two very good musicians played the polka and even stones would be close to giving a yelp if they had heard it. Once the waitress left the room, Earl Rasnov got up.

"I'll just turn it down a bit, otherwise we'll all have to go to bed soon."

"When was the last show of this group? I can't remember." Ralph was very likeable, and he looked more likeable, in his blue T-shirt with his boy next door looks, just with more muscles.

"'Must be Magic' was stopped after two weeks because of my daughter's accident."

The awkward question was so well placed, no one became suspicious.

"How's Frederik? My colleague said he wasn't responsive anymore in the afternoon." Ralph tried to evaluate their mood and despite saying that he just wanted to visit the group, he tried to stay professional.

"He still doesn't feel too well. I gave him his pills. Did he go to bed, Rasno?" asked Bianca.

Ralph noticed Bianca massaging her hands. He thought that she must be nervous because of the condition her husband was in.

"Yes, he's not the same since the accident," explained Earl Rasnov. There was a shimmer in his eyes, and it looked like he'd just got an idea.

"Natalia caused a trauma in all of us. It seems to be the worst for Frederik," said Benny.

"Frederik wants Benny to substitute him in the 'Bloody soirée'." Earl Rasnov surprised everyone.

"Dad, we should've talked about this before. Why do you have to spring surprises on me so much?"

"Don't cry. Frederik can teach you what to do. He's not well." Bianca seemed quite sad about that news, but it could also be her relief. She seemed more relaxed.

"How do you like hanging out with a group like ours?" Ignez pushed Pavel aside and sat down between him and Ralph.

"It's very exciting. What exactly is Frederik's illness?" Ralph couldn't stop himself from asking.

"It's a compulsion neurosis. He must've got it from the trauma of the accident. Natalia and Frederik had the most problems with it. I don't know much about her depressions, but a lot about Frederik's neurosis. He blamed himself for a few months, but now with the right medication, he's become more stable." Bianca seemed to know a lot about this.

"There's always people who blame themselves and suffer more than others. He was too close to the accident; I can understand his unfortunate shock," agreed Ralph.

"Frederik threatened Natalia after the accident. I can remember it very well," said Ignez in a conspiratorial voice.

"That's not right," protested Bianca.

"Right. He said she planned the accident," said Virginia.

"Nonsense. He was shocked and just talked bullshit. I wouldn't bet on what he said," said Bianca in defence of her husband.

"No. He really said that she should be hit by the lamp," insisted Ignez.

"Please, let's change the topic. I can't hear it anymore," said Bianca, who seemed very tired.

✦

When I heard how proud Ralph was of his news from the day before, I got mad. Without my consent, the boy had gone to one of the meetings of those actors and turned all of my investigation upside down. I could imagine him feeling very welcome in a group like theirs in his tight trousers and combed hair.

I had to admit that he told me a few things I probably overheard while questioning Otto. Natalia was an opportunist and by faking her pregnancy, she quarrelled with Frederik and Otto. I didn't know about Frederik's rapture on the day Elmira died, and I didn't think of the possibility of investigating Elmira's death again. I was wrong when I suspected that an accident like this could really happen. As Ralph found out, the vine for the dancers was attached on the wrong position on the stage. From there, the vine pulled down one of the lamps and that's when the accident happened.

But if Natalia changed her position with Elmira on purpose, it would be murder.

The costume which was apparently ripped was the reason for them to change position, however, there was no torn costume, as Helene confirmed.

No one admitted responsibility for attaching the rope to the wrong place, and there was nothing about it in the report of my colleague from the insurance company either. The only thing it said in there was about the possibility of a stagehand maybe attaching the vines in the wrong spot. Ralph learned that Elmira had hung the rope up herself. She was a very good climber and had managed to do it without a ladder.

Ralph also reported that Natalia was not a good climber at all. She had failed a few times when she tried.

I lit another cigarette and puffed the blue smoke through the window. Ms Hiersemann would be mad at me tomorrow, but I didn't care. I felt like I had overlooked so much, I could just leave my job anyway.

The head of the group could have killed Natalia out of revenge as well. He was old, but anyone could strangle the woman by using a leather rope.

'Brr,...' I said to myself and it made me shiver thinking about him turning up in a train dressed as a horror clown. I hate clowns and I had never understood why people think they're funny.

Ralph should have taken me. I would have got more information from this group. I was sure about it.

The Spanish lady didn't have an alibi and I didn't want to spoil things with her. She seemed to be a termagant and was Elmira's best friend. Ralph excluded money as a motive, but I wanted to follow my own thoughts.

The theory of Natalia reading the wrong time on her damaged invitation was something Ralph agreed with and the laboratory confirmed it. Natalia really wasn't the brightest and she had ripped the envelope open on the wrong side. I had overlooked Otto's assertion as well, however, it was stated in Ralph's notes.

I even read the text message and I could have asked the laboratory for it.

'Beginner's luck,' I assumed.

It was late already. I started preparing for the interviews with the suspects and I didn't want to let Ralph get away with solving this case. Somehow his way annoyed me now, although I liked it in the beginning.

If Ralph was right and Natalia was really the reason for Elmira's death, it would most likely be Earl Rasnov, his son and the Spanish lady who had probably killed Natalia.

However, there were other possibilities as well.

'What if they're all part of this?' I thought. In the end, they're all actors.

The bloody soirée

Everyone received an exact summons with information about the place, the time and more about the case and false statements. Inspector Vingard was not very friendly when he handed out the official papers during breakfast. He didn't seem too fond of the information which Ralph found out the day before. When handing out the summons he just drily said: "Don't be late. We want you to be on time, fifteen minutes before the appointment."

Inspector Vingard did not get much praise for this appearance and every actor who disliked him before, liked him even less now.

At noon Otto arrived together with Pavel and Benny in Garmisch. They all looked slightly sad and insecure. After the registration of their personal data, they waited for a while in the anteroom, until a blonde woman called Hiersemann asked Otto to come in.

Inspector Vingard joined them with a few folders and notes and let everything fall on the table while acting very theatrically.

"Oh man! If I hadn't been awake, I would've had a heart attack," moaned Otto.

"You should know that we're looking for answers and I hope you realise it is in your interest to co-operate," said Inspector Vingard in a slightly threatening and challenging manner. Ralph's eyes widened because of this inappropriate behaviour by his colleague.

"You say you didn't know about your wife confusing the time of her arrival. Why did you not react at all?" Inspector Vingard got up while he spoke, and Ralph let him know by the look on his face how horrible his behaviour was.

"Natalia did things like this all the time. She confused times, places and topics. She wasn't very bright. She managed to survive because of how naïve she was. That's just how it was. As soon as she realized that I'd leave her soon, she tried to get my attention all the time, however I just ignored her. But I didn't have a reason to kill her." Otto seemed quite annoyed.

"Oh please, I can promise you, you're not the suspect here. It's just the case that every one of you has information which Inspector Vingard here needs." Ralph was obviously more skilful, and Otto relaxed.

Inspector Vingard turned red, but managed a smile, even if it was just a crooked one.

"Thank you. I'll do this here myself. You're sure Pavel didn't notice this text message at all? Maybe he heard or saw something?" suggested Vingard.

"If you're so curious, we were busy with ourselves and I'm certain you don't want me to show you any proof of that." Otto turned from being a peaceful musician into a threatening creature once he realised that Vingard wanted to go against his Pavel. Vingard blushed even more strongly and smiled shyly once he finally understood what Otto meant.

"Calm down. He doesn't mean it. It was just another piece of information. However, it's good that they were together the whole time. May I ask something about the death of Elmira?" asked Ralph.

"Sure."

"Let's say Natalia caused the accident with the lamp," suggested Ralph.

"What? Natalia? How?"

"Well, Natalia claimed to have a torn costume, however there was no damaged one. At the last minute, she changed position with Elmira. The video recording of the stage was turned off. There are too many signs, aren't there? You can imagine that one could suggest that there's something wrong." Ralph looked at Vingard who stood fuming in the corner of the room, staring at the walls.

"I can't deny it. It could be a possibility. But how are you going to prove this theory?" Otto tried to think about how they should find any evidence.

"It should be us asking the questions here, shouldn't it?" hissed Vingard.

Otto shrugged and didn't answer.

"One last question for today. Were Elmira and Ignez dating?" asked Ralph.

"No, Elmira was hetero and very picky."

"What about Frederik?" added Vingard.

"For me and my sister, Frederik was always more like an uncle. If he'd ever tried to come closer to my sister, my dad would have killed him. Never, ever!" Benny was sure about this.

Vingard had to think about how pale and skinny Earl Rasnov was and for a minute, he saw him looking like a clown. He shivered.

"Thank you, Mr Grossbeck. We'll see you soon, in case we have any further questions." said Ralph.

Otto closed the door behind him and Vingard exploded in the room.

"I'm the one who is head of the questioning. You're a guest here. Don't interfere or I'll send you out again!"

Ralph didn't look very impressed when he looked at Vingard.

"Should I ask the next one to come in?"

Bianca entered the police station and saw Pavel and Otto talking. They sat on chairs which looked old-fashioned and equally impractical. Her face showed how tired she was and how much the constant care for Frederik strained her. She cheered herself up and approached the group confidently.

"This man has a temper," said Pavel so condescendingly and so loudly, everyone in the room could hear it. "I don't know what he wants from us. He's focused on solving the case by pressuring us. What an idiot!" Otto was very upset.

"I'd like to be next. I have to get back to Frederik; he's with your father," whispered Bianca and indicated to both men to be quiet.

"If we can make it work, I'd be happy to let you go first." Pavel's big hand gently touched Bianca's arm.

"Ouch!" she screamed.

"Did I hurt you?" asked Pavel, surprised.

"That was quite harsh! Ouch!" she moaned. Pavel let go of Bianca and distanced himself.

"Did you fix your costume? Helene still hasn't fixed my waistcoat," cried Pavel.

"I'll be the snake lady. We haven't used the faux-silk snake for years and you can do really cool light effects with it. Rasno's idea to be something from the swamps wasn't challenging enough for me," explained Bianca.

"Our *conferencier*[1] Frederik comes together with Ralph from his questioning," Pavel informed them in a gossiping way.

"Thank you for coming. We'll continue with Pavel," said Ralph.

"Could Bianca go first? She'll have to look after Frederik," asked Otto.

---

[1] Show-master

"Sure," answered Ralph, without asking Vingard.

Bianca went into the room and noticed an unpleasant smell.

"Let's get some fresh air in here," suggested Ralph who knew how bad Vingard could smell.

"How can I help?" asked Bianca.

Vingard looked at Ralph. who closed the window again and took over the conversation.

"Natalia must've died at around seven forty-five, plus or minus half an hour. Because of rush hour, the train must have been very busy and until now we couldn't ask anyone for information. Where were you at that time?" Vingard didn't know much about interrogations like these and murder cases weren't very common in Upper Bavaria either. But he didn't want to ask for help from his colleagues in Munich.

"Can you determine the time that precisely?" asked Bianca.

"Not quite, but we know the time the victim got on the train and she should've arrived in Eschenlohe at this time, plus or minus ten minutes. So, where were you?" insisted Ralph.

"I had to be at 'Am Platzl'. There's a small bakery and I wanted to go to the pharmacy which opens at eight, so I could take my time." Bianca quickly looked inside her purse and got out a paper tissue.

"Do you have any receipts or a confirmation for us from this time which could help us?" Ralph looked in the direction of Vingard, who liked the question and nodded approvingly.

"Who asks for a receipt in a bakery at that time? But I can remember the bells of St. Peter's Church, I think. I'm not sure. Fred was asleep and I would've never taken him shopping with me. I'm clueless now."

Vingard nodded towards Ralph and knew that this was enough reason for this timing for now.

"Let's change the topic. What was your role in the show 'Must be Magic' last season?" Ralph tried to be especially sensitive.

"Magician with a bit of trapeze. I flew up in the air and vanished. This was my most important role. It was before the accident. I was in the wardrobe already when the light fell. I just heard it breaking and screams. When I came on stage, I only saw Otto and Pavel who tried to get my husband away from hitting Natalia. Back then, he thought she did it." Bianca's hands were trembling from how exhausted she was and from looking after Frederik, however the tissue helped her to calm down.

"Do you think he was right?" Vingard followed Ralph precisely on how he was leading this questioning and couldn't find a reason why he didn't like what he heard.

"Possibly. But nothing he said since the accident makes sense. He even said it was his fault. I think it's because of the trauma and that's not really a basis for the truth," said Bianca resignedly.

When she left the room, Ralph slammed the door behind her.

"I can see enough reasons why Elmira's death could be murder. I think we should take on the case again." Vingard listened closely and nodded.

"Yes, this could've been a reason to seek for revenge on Natalia as well."

"I can't say who it is that wants revenge the most," said Ralph unintentionally.

✦

The inn seemed to be empty. The Asian waiter wasn't there, and neither was the landlady. All the others received a summons and went to Garmisch when Frederik decided to go outside on the balcony. He took some coffee from a flask and tried to get his bearings. The strong medication calmed him down, but it didn't solve the problems he had to deal with as, for example, his perception and the hallucinations which were getting worse.

He tried to remember what happened on the day Natalia died and everything was just fine according to his obsession with order. Bianca went shopping and he organised his mail and checked the script of the 'Bloody soirée'. He met Bianca at the station, and they drove to Eschenlohe. However, there was one detail which troubled him. Why did he not have any memories of midday or before?

'Everything in one second? What did you do?' The racking voice tried to help him organise his thoughts.

When Elmira died, he was in shock and unconscious for almost six days. He could remember hearing about this.

Since then, he had to deal with a lack of memory and mental blanks every day and he couldn't talk to anyone. He was scared that one day he'd be locked up in a clinic and that would be the end of him. Back in the day, he was a man every woman looked at and everyone wanted. He was the MC of Earl Rasnov. He should be the hangman in the new show, but right now he felt more like the victim on the scaffold than the hangman.

The racking voice had become more present during the last months and turned almost into something like a friend. This voice was at least something that helped him remember how everything was connected.

What did he see when Elmira died?

The audience was cheering while he encouraged them to see both dancers. Both graces wore faux-feather hats made out of the finest tissue paper. Earl Rasnov never used any products containing anything derived from animals. Even the ropes for the trapeze were made of hard cotton.

"Hard cotton?" said Frederik loudly.

Suddenly he remembered something. Something he saw which scared him even more.

'Why are you scared of cotton? You sheep!' joked the demon.

His body trembled and he felt insecure. He looked for his phone. He needed to call Bianca. He needed help. The feeling in his stomach got worse and he had to breathe faster.

'What did you do?'

Further away, there was a car driving up the mountain way to the inn.

Frederik remembered his last conversation with Natalia before Elmira's last performance.

"I don't care if you're pregnant or not. It's your problem if you try to hit on men, you should take the Pill or use something else. Talk to Rasno, but I'm not responsible for you." Frederik could hear himself talking to her. His voice and the voice of the demon mixed to become a creepy choir.

The car parked and two officers got out. One of them wore a sophisticated dark blue suit and the other one a mixture of offers from the mall which disturbed Frederik's sense of organisation.

"If you can't see the markings on the floor and can't remember where you're supposed to stand then leave it to someone who can!" screamed Frederik to Natalia.

'You're mean. You're a murderer.' The demon became visible again and the world turned pink in front of his eyes.

Both officers approached him and said something he didn't understand. He tried to use his phone, but he couldn't hold on to it, so it fell to the floor.

"We'll take you. Don't worry," said the man who went shopping in the mall.

"He seemed like he didn't understand. Take his phone and call his wife or someone else. Tell them we'll take him to the hospital," ordered the pseudo-manager.

His smile seemed wider than normal.

Frederik didn't offer resistance and got up, kind of thankful that someone was here to help him.

"One moment, please. Where?" Frederik managed to say.

"We want to take you to the hospital. There you'll get help."

"Who are you?" Frederik paused for a minute and waited for an explanation.

"Earl Rasnov asked us to help you," mumbled the one from the mall.

In this moment Frederik looked at his hands and he realized that he knew something, but he could recall it. Then he found himself sitting in the car, waiting for them to drive off.

Frederik looked at his hands again and tried to remember. His new demon friend said 'Those hands are the hands of a hangman. And Earl Rasnov knows it.'

✦

Two women sat in a bistro close to the police station and waited for another friend of the acting group. Virginia and Helene watched Hugo, who was inspecting the bushes close by.

Despite her impressive clothes and hair dos, Virginia looked resigned. Her sadness was hidden behind a mask of relief and she smiled at Helene happily.

"You really want to leave me and the group?" she asked and quickly sipped on her coffee.

"It's better like this. We got stuck and I don't know another solution for my work in Berlin." Helene sounded relieved after she mentioned the inevitable goodbye.

"Did you tell Rasno about it?" Virginia picked up Hugo from the ground.

"He more or less arranged all of it and agreed with Berlin that both of us were betrayed by Natalia. No one knows where my money ended up and especially not Otto apparently. Rasno offered to take part of the expenses, but the condition was for me to take on this work in Berlin for one whole year. And I want a change of scenery. I'm sorry." Helene stroked Hugo's head.

"He'll miss you."

"I don't think so. He just listens to what you're saying, and he only came to me for food. He doesn't like sleeping close to me either. Rasno doesn't know who will replace me yet. Apparently, he has a few new applications I should look at." Helene gazed into nothing and the past seemed to vanish. She knew that this also included Virginia now, but she knew this moment had been coming for a long time. However, she lacked the courage to actually face this day.

"I know. I'll train the newbies." Virginia knew that this work was a milestone in her career, as she turned from being the youngest member of the group, into the leader of the new members.

"What will we do with our apartment? Half of it is your workshop," said Virginia.

"The apartment isn't that expensive, and half of my workshop is full of your costumes. It's not a problem. I'll just take my tools and personal things with me. I'll leave the rest to you. I still don't understand why they asked me to come here for this useless questioning by the police. They wanted to know where I was, exactly what I did, but I could prove everything on my phone. I just wanted the money from Natalia. No matter if she was dead or alive, it wouldn't have changed anything. I still need the money." The latent anger in her voice was very obvious.

"If 'The bloody soirée' is successful and if I earn some money, I can send you some." Virginia quickly tried to calculate it in her head; however, she doubted her mathematic skills but didn't want to say anything.

"No, I want a clean cut and nothing I have to depend on," said Helene confidently.

"But we'll stay friends, won't we?"

"Sure. Who would like to get in trouble with an axe lady like you?"

"Not even a werewolf like you." They laughed about their roles in the 'Bloody soirée'.

"Right. It won't be a problem to find another scene designer, however finding a new werewolf will be hard. It's an important role in the 'Bloody soirée'. It's part of the draft of the posters." Helene went through the other team members but doubted that any of them could take on this role.

"I can't do both parts. I couldn't manage it timewise. When are you leaving?"

Helene stared into space and knew what she wanted to say, but she couldn't find the right words immediately.

"I'll go to Berlin at the end of the week. Could you please send my things there once I know my address?" Virginia nodded and tried to understand the new situation.

"Oh man! So early?" Virginia could feel herself being close to tears for one moment and she looked for comfort in the sleeping Hugo who sat on her lap.

"After this incident I don't think I like this group very much anymore. Two dead people and one man who apparently goes crazy. That's too much for me. I'd rather leave the group before I'm next. I'll pay off my debt in Berlin with the money I'll earn. That'll be over in ten weeks and after that I have a few orders from smaller and independent productions. All of that is a positive development for me." Helene was happy with the scenario in her head and apparently didn't want to deal with Virginia's feelings anymore.

"Do you think it could be someone of the group who is responsible for those incidents?" asked Virginia with her eyes wide open.

"I don't know. I thought about it myself and found reasons with every one of us to kill Natalia. Well? Except Benny. Wait. He could've hated her because of his sister. I didn't think about the thing with the change of their positions until now. But Elmira's death is a mystery to all of us. Everyone liked her a lot." Helene didn't exclude herself from the group who was very contemptuous of what happened to Natalia.

"That's tight. We still hope that it was someone unknown who didn't receive their payment and killed her because of it. She didn't have any money but probably plenty of debt. Otto told me that every one of us paid money to Natalia to support the theatre," said Virginia, remembering the conversation from the night before.

"Apparently, one of us paid for another reason. I'm sure Natalia was involved in both cases. No matter what."

✦

'Don't get mixed up with an angry woman,' thought Earl Rasnov as an angry Bianca stood in front of him. She had her hands on her waist and looked him deep in his eyes.

"What did you think, deciding something like this without talking to me first?" It was clearly not a question but a complaint. Benny was sitting next to his father and wanted to stay out of this discussion. He put his notebook aside and got up quietly.

"Stay here! I want to talk to you as well." Benny stood still immediately after Bianca's command. Bianca raised her finger as he wanted to sigh because of how annoyed he was.

"Don't you dare! I'm warning you!" she shouted.

"I talked to Frederik about its last night. He asked me if I could take him to hospital without making it a big thing. That's not the first time this happened. Last year, and the year before, he asked me to do the same thing," explained Earl Rasnov.

"And you dare to get me out of the house for a few hours to take Frederik to the hospital against my will? I hope you're aware that I'll go there today, get him out and sue you afterwards!" Her threats became louder and her voice higher.

Benta watched Frederik without saying anything and signalled to her daughter to keep an eye on what was happening here.

"Calm down. He just didn't want to talk to you about his feelings. Sometimes husbands don't want to seem so weak in front of their wives. We're almost one family. I guess you should respect him for choosing me to talk to, shouldn't you?" Rasno tried to sound rational, but he knew that he dared too much.

Ignez came closer to the discussion and watched closely what happened.

For one short moment Bianca pushed her fingers on her eyes to try to keep her temper.

"He's still my husband and I want to look after him. Do you know what they'll do to him in a place like this? Do you know how it'll be to live with someone who acts like a brainless monkey? No, you don't. No one asked for you to interfere in the lives of others and as soon as it gets chaotic, you're gone. Where were you, as his best friend, when I needed you during the last two years? When he was unconscious for six days? Where were you?" demanded Bianca.

"Bianca, you're upset, and you don't know what you're saying. I did everything I could to help Fred, but I can't heal his spirit," said Rasno, trying to apologise.

"I suppose you know a lot about spirits. You talk to them on stage, but this is real life and here is your talent just a fraud and nothing else. I don't agree with you doing this behind my back!" Bianca was in a rage but at the same time she didn't want to overstrain herself for the upcoming questioning with the police.

"The doctor is a friend of mine and he promised me not to give Frederik any pills without asking you first. He's there for a short check-up and a mental evaluation. Frederik was desperate and he's like a brother to me. Please try to understand," asked Earl Rasnov.

Benny seized the opportunity to run from all of this and tried to get away without attracting any attention.

"I can understand your father, but I can't forgive you. I always treated you as if you were my nephew, and you betray me like this? How dare you?"

"Bianca, I'm sorry, but I just did what my father asked me to and that's always my main priority." Benny had never fallen out with Bianca before and tried to avoid any confrontation at all. However, not to respect his father's wishes could cause more problems than enduring the short-lived anger of Bianca.

Ignez and Benta watched their conversation without saying a word and acted like they'd been reading the newspaper. At the same time, Ignez saw Virginia saying goodbye to Helene and how Virginia and Hugo came back to the house. Pavel was with the police and hadn't noticed anything of what happened here. But Benta promised him, right before he went inside, to report everything he missed.

"Both of you should take notes now. If I have to go back to Munich with a dead zombie as my husband, Natalia's death will be the least of your problems. And me performing in the 'Bloody soirée' is something that belongs to the past. You can look for someone else!"

Earl Rasnov's phone vibrated as he received a text message which said: 'I remembered, and I have to talk to you.'

Earl Rasnov showed it to his son and both of them watched Bianca slamming the door behind her. She left the group after this big show of hers and left two men behind who sat there and were deeply embarrassed.

Frederik was almost thirty kilometres away in his hospital bed and had a doctor checking his blood and heart rate. Frederik could hear the voice in his head sounding like an echo.

'I'll see you in hell.'

✦

Ralph and his other colleagues went through Natalia's finances while everyone else was in Garmisch. They especially noticed some members of the group paying more money than others. Sometimes, Natalia transferred the money to a third party with an identical reference.

His colleagues collected the names of the recipients who Natalia transferred money to and on another list, they wrote down where Natalia received her money from. They spent the whole night doing this and the first shift had already said goodbye to them.

Ms Hiersemann had been in the office for twenty hours already and refused to leave. She slept on the couch in the storage room and looked very ruffled when she came out of it.

"Margot, please, go home. You look horrible," said Ralph, trying to cheer her up.

"You too, dear. What did the children of the IT department find out?" she asked. She brushed her hair and pulled her clothes straight. She was in her early forties and not married as her career had always been more important than her private life.

"Natalia, the victim, believed she'd be the new star. She spent massive amounts of money on marketing. I called the two most expensive ones and figured out that they both took advantage of how naïve their victim was. One of the people who received most of her money was a healer. Excuse me, but in my opinion, this healer stole Natalia blind. She paid bills which were higher than what I earn in a year, for three months in a row. Useless appointments with photographers, articles in unknown newspapers, dodgy therapies and one journey for a casting, which had definitely nothing to do with her work. She paid a lot of money to a moderator on the radio, just for him to tell her that she'd never have a chance of an interview. She simply paid him to put her name into the programme once. Reading all of this, I have to say I think this woman was absolutely stupid," summarised Ralph.

"Before I went to bed here, I could hear Vingard running around here, saying the husband and his monster are like Dracula and his footman. He thinks they're murderers. The laughter in the room brought him down and he misbehaved slightly again. I'm sorry you have to work on this case with him, but I suppose in the field we're working in, we can't choose who we want to work with," said Ms Hierseman apologetically.

"Not them nor their behaviour. He's a homophobe and very conservative. I doubt he'll ever change. I don't care. I'm sure we shouldn't trace back the information about the victim anymore. It's obvious that she was above herself and I think she must've been in a condition ready for treatment and hospital already. It'd be down to them not drawing a line between affection and psychological behaviour in their business. The husband just ignored everything and that's all he is guilty of. Sad." Ralph got out the list with her income and looked through the amounts of money.

"Frederik and Bianca were her biggest supporters. According to your notes, he dated Natalia once and she faked a pregnancy after. Maybe that's why he paid her more than the others. Sometimes men are just naïve. Sorry, I didn't want to aim this towards you." It was too late when Ms Hiersemann realised her lack of sensibility and literally just said what she was thinking about.

"It doesn't matter. I think so too. I'll still ask them all for their reasons to pay her. Who's in there right now?" Ralph sounded almost curious.

"The husband and the Spanish women are next. The younger one is extremely good looking. My dear God. But if I had to guess, if she were the murderer, she would've picked another way to kill Natalia. Strangling a victim is too personal," commented Margot.

"She lost money because of Natalia. However, I don't see a reason for something like this. I'll let you know when I'm done questioning them."

"Did Vingard agree to you being in there as well?" she asked.

"My boss arranged it with the head of the department. I'll manage. Vingard won't like it but that's what he has to deal with."

"Go on then. We'll all like that."

Both of them laughed.

✦

Inspector Vingard seemed to be haunted. With every interview he just witnessed even crazier people or stories. They were people he would've chosen not to meet. And his new colleague Ralph turned out to be the new favourite of Ms Hiersemann. He couldn't ignore them chatting away whenever he left the room with a red face or whenever another colleague laughed at him. His prejudices and ideals belonged to a time of change which he only knew from TV shows where he always had the opportunity to turn them off. However, in reality, getting used to such changes had a lot of friction loss.

Benta introduced herself and her daughter and clearly stated that there wouldn't be any questioning without her being there. Inspector Vingard could hardly understand her swearing and cursing. The only Spanish he knew was from two holidays in Mallorca. He had tried to avoid the subject in school.

Vingard looked at both women. He exhaled deeply and for the first time, he could feel some normality in the group.

'At last, a tall, slender and beautiful woman with her loving mother,' he thought and was happy to relax a bit.

"Thank you for taking the time to talk to me," he mumbled, leaning over the protocol which was in front of him.

"We have to rehearse and have a life otherwise as well. We've been here for almost four hours already. I hope you can understand why we're upset. We're not under arrest yet, are we?" said Ignez insistently and the sight of her met Vingard like a hammer out of nowhere.

'Nuisance!' he cursed mentally and couldn't hide his anger.

"I'm sorry, I thought my colleague would help me out … I'll hurry," he lied.

"What questions should we answer if we don't know anything useful anyway?" protested Benta.

Vingard counted down from ten and looked through Ralph's notes.

"We'll see. How would you describe your relationship to the victim Elmira?" He read the first question out loud without looking at the two women.

"Who are you talking to? Lift your chin and look at the person you are talking to. Did you not learn how to behave?" Benta's full authority forced him to apologise.

'Oh God!' he cursed in his head.

"Right. Should we start with you?" he asked, overly nice.

The room seemed a lot smaller and he tried to regain his authority and to calm down their protests by asking his question.

"She was like a daughter to me. I'm very close to Earl Rasnov and Elmira even spent a few holidays with me and Ignez. We were like a *famiglia*. What do you know about the accident?" asked Benta.

"Nothing so far. Please, it's me who asks question here, isn't it?" Vingard was asking for respect. "How close are you to Earl Rasnov?" Vingard asked Benta.

Ignez looked at him confusedly and spread out her hands.

"They're in love, you should know that. They have sex and the only reason they're not a couple yet is that Rasno is not quite over the death of his former wife. I hope I don't have to draw you a picture as well." Ignez laughed.

"Ignez! Please!" Benta warned her daughter.

Vingard summarised what she had just said and just wrote down one word.

"And you?" he asked, inviting Ignez to continue.

"We were best friends and shared a lot of secrets through our teenage years. It was a shock for me to lose her. We met through Pavel and got along well from the beginning. If I found out that it was Natalia who killed her, I would've slit her open myself."

'Aggressive,' he summarised.

"And that's no joke!" Ignez added.

'Dangerous,' he wrote down before 'aggressive'.

"Ditto," said Benta and nodded.

"A lot of strength is needed to strangle a person. That's why you're not suspects in this case. Natalia was strangled with a strap from her suitcase." Vingard tried to sound professional.

"Nonsense. It's a strap from the trapeze. I saw a picture and immediately recognized it. Even my mother could strangle her. A strap like this can hold more than three hundred kilos. Do you think it's only men who can be strong?" Ignez pointed on the picture of the victim and showed him the pattern on the throat.

"No, of course not. Please, I apologise. Are you sure about it?" Vingard seemed like he realised something and could finally present a result from these questions.

"Sure. I took one as well. It's definitely the pattern of the strap. I mean, why did you not realise it? The police were at the theatre as well." Ignez didn't realise that she had made herself a suspect as well.

"So the perpetrator could be someone from your group or someone who works at the theatre? Who else has access to straps like this?" Vingard was excited and looked through the glass window towards the office and looked at his colleague.

Benta signalled to Ignez to be careful. But there was no going back for Ignez.

"Those straps are where the props are, right next to the stage on the left side. Now I remember." Ignez lifted her long, skinny fingers in front of her mouth.

"What's wrong?" asked Vingard who was obviously very excited.

"Natalia and Elmira used straps like these for their dance on the vines. Natalia probably took hers back then. She liked to steal props," summarised Ignez.

Vingard knocked on the table and made both women jump.

"I read your chronological records, and everything makes sense if you don't support each other. I hope you understand that your alibis are not strong enough, however right now I just want to understand how everything could happen." Vingard wrote down the fact that the said strap belonged to the theatre.

Vingard wasn't quite satisfied with his questioning yet and he wondered how he could find out even more. When Benta started impatiently tapping her small feet on the floor, he realised he had thought for too long.

"Did one of you have something with Frederik as well?" Vingard added.

Ignez laughed loudly and too affectionately.

"You seem to underestimate us. *Madre* would've slapped him if he came closer to her. He respects us too much," said Ignez emphatically.

Vingard was sure that he'd never want to mess with these two harmless-looking women.

"I mean, well … he's not ugly and I just wanted to know if one of you maybe ever had something with him. Please don't misunderstand me."

"You're not a good observer, are you?" Benta surprised him.

"What do you mean?" mumbled Vingard.

"My daughter is a lesbian," Benta said, seeking revenge on her daughter.

✦

The questioning with the inspector ended earlier than expected and according to his posture, he didn't expect what Benta said about Ignez. Both left the room with big smiles on their faces and left a shocked officer behind them. It could be classified as childish behaviour, but he was so cold and very unfriendly to Pavel and Otto and everyone in the group knew about it. So they all decided to make him pay.

Both ladies went back to the group and looked around.

"Who's next?" asked Bianca.

"No one wants to talk to me. Apparently, they approved my alibi and as Natalia wasn't killed by an axe or a throwing knife, no one thinks I could be the murderer. However, if I think about it, I would've liked to get this bitch out of her grave, revive her and cut her into pieces. Even after her death she's still a pain in the arse," said Virginia.

"Be careful what you're saying here. The walls have ears here," warned Otto.

"I don't care. If I killed someone, I would dissolve her in acid. Helene left me for good and moved to Berlin." There was an obvious disappointment in her voice. Ignez seemed uncertain on how she should act, so she just nodded.

"How do you feel, Virginia? It must've been a big shock for you," said Benta sympathetically.

"We knew it for a long time, but just decided not to face the truth. I will miss her, but now I can at least focus on a new future. I was always more the relationship-type girl of us." Virginia's disappointment was clear, even if she didn't want to show it.

"I think that's a good trait. It can ruin your character and the way to happiness to change the partner too often. I've been living with Frederik for such a long time now, I don't even know where he starts, and I end anymore. Sometimes I even feel like I have the same illness as him."

Bianca got up and looked into the conference room. She looked at Pavel who sat there clueless.

"Pavel doesn't feel very well."

"What did this man ask?" asked Bianca.

"It was me who realised that Natalia was strangled with a strap from the trapeze. They didn't know the patterns on the side of the rope, but I recognised it immediately, looking at the picture they had. Apparently, Natalia used it to secure her luggage. How cheap of her."

Someone in the group seemed to realise something when Ignez told them about the strap, but no one could say who it was.

"You shouldn't have said it! It could've been other ropes as well. You made us all look guilty," protested Otto.

"But that's how it is. You would've recognized it as well. I just want to know why you didn't tell anyone about it. The inspector told me it was a strap from the suitcase. What an idiot!" said Ignez seemingly confused.

"Nonsense. No one is able to see which pattern it was on her dead body. Well, I've never seen a dead body, but I can only just imagine it." Bianca thought about it for a long time and seemed like she disagreed.

"But the police found Natalia with it, didn't they?" asked Ignez.

"I thought you fell out with Rasno and left?" said Benta, facing Bianca.

"I understand why you're worried. Frederik's really not well. I agreed to leave him in hospital for three days. However, it was the third time now that Rasno tried to get Frederik to hospital without asking me first. And this time he was successful. The first and second meeting after Elmira died, I caught him, and I thought he might have given up on the thought. He's old and persistent. I hope he'll drop it after this now," said Bianca hopefully.

"Vingard asked us where we were and about our relationship to Elmira and Natalia. We didn't lie," Ignez informed them all. She sat down on an old couch which seemed as if it had been green once. Now it looked more like a grey and brown colour, but on some parts of it there were indications of what it once looked like.

"Ralph took Virginia's information and asked us to leave, but we decided to wait for Pavel and Earl Rasnov. They're still in there." Bianca seemed more relaxed.

"Pavel's so scared. He sits in there like a schoolboy. I'd love to be with him right now." Benta had to laugh because of Bianca's motherly instincts.

"Bianca, please. Look how tall he is. If he sneezes too heavily, the inspector would be glued to the wall. But I have to say that he shouldn't wear his stage outfit to such an occasion." Benta thought his outfit was a bit too much for a conversation like this one.

"That's his new brand. He now wears Venolini. That's a designer from Italy who pays him to be his model. It's not a costume," said Virginia.

"Oh my God! That alone is a reason to lock him away. Apparently, they found a connection between Elmira's accident and what happened to Natalia. Do you think that's possible?" asked Ignez.

Everyone looked puzzled and a certain turmoil was in the group, although no one could see it.

"Maybe. I'm afraid, the answer to that question could be important for the future of our 'Bloody soirée' as well," noted Benny who just approached them.

Pavel knew that the inspector didn't like him very much. He probably wanted to lock him away for just any reason. He wore red and yellow trousers and for someone who wasn't into fashion, he looked like he wore a costume. However, everyone who knew him also knew that it was just one of his designer outfits. Inspector Vingard tried hard not to look at his crotch, but the shining fabric was almost like a magnet to his eyes. He was extremely confused and couldn't resist so he skimmed through his papers and turned his chair slightly to the left.

He thought about this situation and knew their relationship would only suffer more if he were to confront Vingard. Despite his efforts to explain that he'd never be able to hurt anyone, the inspector still tried to find out where he could possibly have lied.

"You're familiar with the straps of a trapeze, aren't you?" The inspector asked him as if he already knew the answer.

Pavel thought about what this question could be about and looked cluelessly in the direction of the inspector. At this second, he saw Benta who quickly looked into the room and waved at him.

"Sure, I know them. What's wrong about that?"

"Where do you store them?"

"I don't know. I don't use them. You should know that, shouldn't you? Please, look at me. You should know that a man of my size can't perform a dance with ropes. I spit fire and I can lift two dancers. And sure, I do look impressive. I'm sure you can see it yourself." Pavel pushed his chair back and lifted his right leg slightly. Inspector Vingard was slightly disgusted and looked back at his papers. He turned even further to the left.

"Please look at the pattern here on the throat of the victim. Do you know it?"

Pavel was confused. He didn't know it and neither did he know what the inspector wanted from him.

"I'm sorry, but I'm afraid I can't help you. If Natalia was burnt or squeezed like a worm, I would probably be able to help you more. And anyway, we already know that my partner and I were far, far away from Natalia." Inspector Vingard had to admit that he was right, and he dropped it.

"Yes. You're right. It was just out of habit. How was your relationship with the victim?"

"Elmira?" A short pause followed, and Pavel didn't have to say anything. It was obvious what he felt. This mountain of man looked soft and vulnerable, as if he remembered his best friend.

"Yes, so?" Vingard prompted him.

"Elmira was the best woman I've ever known. She helped me with my coming out. She helped me find trust in myself. It was Elmira who made me the best fiery djinn on any German stages." Pavel sounded proud with a slight hint of pain in his voice. He felt tears coming up to honour Elmira. Vingard could clearly see how painful this was for Pavel. He wanted to avoid feeling sorry for him and after an internal struggle, he continued by asking another question.

"Coming what?"

"I committed to my sexual orientation and I didn't have to continue living a secret life. Elmira didn't have any prejudices, she was wise and even smarter than her brother, I guess. They both almost wasted their talent during shows, but Earl Rasnov was keen on providing a good education for his geniuses." Vingard listened and thought about what he had just heard. It was so obvious to see that his head was working really hard to connect all the dots.

"I'm not good with linguistics, but I think I understand. You say you were really good friends. What did you mean by geniuses? That's the part I don't understand," said Vingard.

"Elmira was more than that. She was like my sister, the woman I trusted and the one by my side. I miss her a lot. She and her brother went to a school for highly talented children. They have a very high IQ, however, according to Earl Rasnov, they were just normal children."

Vingard's eyes sparkled, as if he finally found something of interest.

"What would you have done if you'd figured out that Natalia was the reason for Elmira to die? Would you have lost your temper? Would you seek revenge?"

Pavel turned red and his eyes became even redder for a short moment.

"Were Benny's suspicions accurate?" Pavel's voice grew to a loud thunder which made the room shake. Vingard started to feel scared.

"Maybe. We're not that far. What would you have done?" Vingard wanted to provoke Pavel into confessing what he had done.

"I think Natalia wouldn't have survived this confrontation. However, before me, Earl Rasnov would've sorted it," summarised Pavel. Vingard was surprised and disappointed at the same time.

"How would he have done it if he had done it? Just in theory."

"I'll never say anything against Earl Rasnov. I'm sure if he did it, no one would ever find out. He's too intelligent."

✦

Earl Rasnov was alone in the cafeteria thinking about his meeting with Inspector Vingard when Benta entered the room.

"Rasno. What are you doing here? We're all upstairs waiting for you. We want to know how it went. No one really likes Inspector Vingard. I really don't understand how someone as stupid as him can work here." She sat next to him and let him feel a bit of her affection.

"I'm old. I should never have agreed to this idea Benny had. I feel like I'm the one who's responsible for Natalia's death." He looked sad. Benta realised that his coffee was ice cold and not drinkable anymore. She went to get him a new one and a piece of cake with it.

"Here. This will cheer you up."

"I'd rather have one of your Magdalenas." Earl Rasnov smiled and Benta felt better.

"That's nonsense. What happened to Natalia is her own fault. She played with fire for too long. Otto told me about the sums of money which she spent for useless advertisement agencies and healers. We would've kicked her out of the group after this meeting anyway." Benta looked towards the door, but no one had come looking for them yet.

"Ignez told Vingard about the pattern on Natalia's throat and that it is the same as the patterns on our trapeze straps."

"Yes. I was there."

"Vingard asked me if I had the same opinion. I knew that it was one of us who was responsible for her death when I said it. The new actors didn't know Natalia and every one of us had a few of those straps, as well as other props. My accountant remembers everything. I just gave them to you without saying anything and noted them as a loss in my papers. I didn't want to have another vine dance in one of my shows. I'm just scared that Benny's right and Elmira's death wasn't an accident and that it could blow up our whole group now. The 'Bloody soirée' depends on the results of this investigation." Benta listened carefully and tried to think about a way to help out. For a few seconds, she seemed clueless.

"I'm old as well, Rasno. However, I wonder how long you'll be sad because of your dead wife. Are we ever going to be together or will I die on my own? Ignez will move out eventually. We're been together for so many years already, there's not much left, is there?" Benta came closer to Earl Rasnov, who took her hands thankfully and gently.

"You'll never be old. You're my Desert Flower who'll live forever. Looking at you, I can only see the Benta who always looked after me and gave me so much. I think you're right. We should think about this part of our future as well. I don't want to continue a life without you, and my ex-wife has been dead for so long, I can hardly remember her."

"Ignez just told Vingard about it. But I took revenge and told Vingard she's a lesbian. You know how much she hates it." Both of them laughed. "You should've told me about it."

"About what?"

"About what Benny said. Did you think you had to investigate alone?" Benta snuggled herself in Rasnov's side.

"Well, we all thought Frederik would remember the accident once we were all together and started the rehearsals for the 'Bloody soirée'. We wanted to confront Natalia because we found out that her costume was never ripped. All of this seemed fine, however, now I feel like I condemned Natalia too early and never gave her a chance to defend herself."

"Did you tell Vingard about it?" Benta went with her fingers through Earl Rasnov's hair and he let her beguile him.

"He realised it himself and after what Helene and Benny told him, he was sure that Elmira's accident was Natalia's fault. He wants to question Frederik as well."

"Why did you let Frederik be hospitalised?"

"Frederik told me he felt continuously worse since Elmira's accident and that he suffered hallucinations at the moment. He even described to me the small devil who talks to him. This was reason enough for me to help him, without Bianca's agreement. He said his medication was too strong and didn't help either. Bianca is really mad at me, but he's my friend. I did it because he asked me to as well."

"Bianca's not mad, but she is tired and it's just so hard for her to admit that she isn't strong enough to handle Frederik's mental illness anymore. Every woman would feel like this."

Earl Rasnov looked deep into Benta's eyes and held her neck with just one hand.

"Would you like to look after me like this as well?"

Benta's heart started beating more heavily before she agreed by kissing him.

✦

Pavel and Ignez laughed about Vingard's questioning and all the others laughed thinking about him staring at Pavel's crotch. Vingard could hear them and asked Benny to come to the conference room. He stared at the group as evilly as possible. However, this didn't seem to have any impact on them. If anything, Pavel presented his crotch to Ignez who almost died laughing.

"Everyone I already questioned may leave, please!" shouted Vingard. He stood at the doorstep and slammed the door behind him.

Benny had to laugh and did his best to conceal it in front of Vingard.

"I'm sorry, but you have to understand, Pavel is our clown and whenever he gets nervous, he just starts to joke all the time. That's his way of handling problems. It's nothing personal." Benny tried to apologise for the bad behaviour of the group.

"I didn't take it personally anyway" said Vingard as drily as possible. The door banged behind Benny and the group of laughing actors got up and waved at Vingard while they went towards the exit.

"How can I help you with this investigation?"

"Well, as far as I understood, you're the one who's responsible for this meeting." Vingard tried to gain some of his authority back.

"Maybe. For the first six months after my sister died, I didn't set foot in the theatre. And neither did my father. When I decided to work in there again, we suffered a liquidity problem which forced me to take on other work. That's why I didn't have the time to check the theatre thoroughly. The insurance company checked the accident for almost one year and it was eighteen months later when they were done, and we were allowed to go in the theatre again." Benny tried to justify his later actions by telling Vingard everything that happened.

"Investigations like these can take a while for the police as well. I can understand it." As Vingard hadn't got very far with his aggressive strategy, he now tried to sound more co-operative to get as much information as possible.

"The first thing I noticed was Natalia's dress. It wasn't torn after all. I can still remember how much of a show she put on to convince all of us not to face the audience with her right side. Natalia came always up with some ideas which didn't need justifying. And then Frederik. Once, as he called me, he moaned about Natalia always missing her mark on the stage. I looked for the recordings of this day in our studio, but apparently, no one had even started the tape. Normally, we always film our performances."

Vingard sat down and started to think about what Benny was saying.

"When I looked at the recorded files on the computer, I realised that someone had turned it on, however, twelve minutes before the accident happened, someone turned it off again. Whoever it was, it must've been someone who didn't know the computer very well. Otherwise, they could've just deleted the file, and no one would've ever noticed that the recording had been stopped. I have to say, our system is really easy. Natalia's stupidity and clumsiness were clue enough for me to suspect her. However, I couldn't prove it and it wasn't enough for the police, or even just to confront her with it."

Vingard raised his hand in front of his lips, something he always did when he was excited.

"Please continue," he asked and breathed heavily.

"I then checked the vine. It was the one my sister was attached to. I couldn't help noticing that the hook on the alignment was in the wrong place. There are markings for where those ropes should go. My sister wouldn't have missed them. At one point I heard Frederik complaining about Natalia's positioning again. He was in such a rage about her not being on her marking, he didn't realise she was on the completely wrong side. If Natalia only stood on the wrong marking on the other side and my sister remained on the planned side, no one would've been hurt by the falling lamp. I thought this would be a great case of insurance fraud, which would be typical for Natalia." Benny looked at Vingard, who obviously was very interested in what he told him.

"Why did you not tell me this earlier?" Benny shrugged and Vingard gave him a sign to continue his story.

"Yes. That's when my father and I came up with the theory that Natalia maybe tampered with the hook. We also realised that we would only ever find out the truth if everyone was in the theatre, helping to clarify the accident. And I wanted to confront Natalia," concluded Benny.

"Did Natalia know about this?"

"I was careless and indicated it during a conversation. I told her I'd like to talk about it with the whole group."

"Did anyone else know about it?"

"No, however Natalia told me that she wanted to clarify what happened. In return, she wanted help with the finances of the dance school."

✦

Frederik arrived with a male nurse straight from the hospital. He protested all the time, as he insisted on being able to walk by himself and not being pushed around as if on a shopping trip.

"Please be quiet. I have to get you to the interview and back to the hospital in one piece. Don't make it harder than it has to be," warned the nurse.

Vingard waved the nurse inside the conference room and was happy when he saw only Bianca sitting in the waiting room. No one else was there who could have laughed at him. Ralph, the new best friend of Ms Hiersemann, didn't even look at him and didn't try to help at all.

"Better like this," mumbled Vingard to himself.

The nurse handed over Frederik while Ralph stood at his side. Vingard closed the door. He didn't want to hear anything about the papers which the nurse had brought with him. They all went straight to Ralph.

"He can do the office work himself," mumbled Vingard again.

"What did you say?" asked Frederik.

"Ah, nothing. I'm just thinking. Sorry for asking you to come here, but at the moment you're the key figure in the story."

"Sounds important." Frederik could hear the door closing behind him and he sat down at the conference table.

"What did you mean when you said that Natalia stood on the wrong marking on the stage?" Vingard felt slightly overwhelmed and he could feel the long day resting on his shoulders.

Frederik quickly thought about it, but his usual demon wasn't there to help him.

"Why does this concern Natalia's death on the train?" he asked.

"Please, I'm the one asking the questions. Just so we stick to the protocol." Vingard hit the right argument with Frederik and he tried to answer the questions correctly.

"When I heard the noise coming from behind the stage, I turned around to see Natalia looking at me with her eyes wide open. It was this moment when I realised that it should've been Elmira standing on her marking."

"So you wanted to see Natalia on the other side of the stage, standing under the falling lamp."

Frederik stopped for a minute. He seemed shocked.

'Got you!' whined the demon.

"No. Why would you say this? It was just a reflex."

"I saw the amounts of money which you transferred to Natalia. My colleague found out that Natalia was in debt, so she couldn't have another bank account. She blackmailed you. Please don't deny it. It'll just cost us time. Natalia tried to blackmail you with her fake pregnancy as well. Combined with everything I heard from her husband, I can see a pattern in the behaviour of the victim. I'll reopen Elmira's case and I'm sure you're the only one who knows the solution to this riddle." Vingard felt his self-confidence coming back.

"Yes, right. I transferred money to Natalia. But how can you prove your allegation?" demanded Frederik as his last resort to regain the power over what just happened.

"Natalia wanted to tell everyone about her trying to hurt Elmira on stage. As many told me, she wasn't very smart, however, she always wrote down what she wanted to say. It needed a lot to interpret what she meant, but it should be enough for a lawsuit. Confess and we'll talk about a trial. If you decide not to confess, you'll find yourself on thin ice. Admit you averted this silly blackmailing because of a fake pregnancy. Her blood should've been checked after an accident like hers, and you would've known if she was pregnant then, wouldn't you?"

Vingard knew he didn't have any proof, but his poker face was perfect. And it looked like it was working. Frederik was tired and didn't have his pills, which made it hard for him to talk. Vingard noticed that as well.

"I just wanted to shock her. I knew she couldn't find the marking on the stage, so it was the safest option to prep the light so it'd fall on this particular marking. However, for some reason, Natalia knew what I wanted to do and decided to change position with Elmira. It was an accident. However, I couldn't tell Rasno about it. We're good friends. If I told him his best friend was indirectly responsible for the death of his daughter, it would've been a tragedy. Please, you have to understand." Frederik sounded desperate and defeated. He seemed to run out of his strength and Vingard made sure the nurse was staying close by. Frederik shivered and it looked like he had to tell the whole story before he became unconscious.

"What happened when Natalia died? Were you responsible for that as well?"

"Nonsense. I can hardly orientate myself. How should I get on a train, find Natalia and kill her? That's just impossible for me. I black out a lot due to my medication. That could be dangerous for me."

"At least you have the best reason to kill her. I will send a guard to the hospital. However, you will have to admit responsibility for Elmira's death and confess in front of the court." Vingard could be happy with himself when he left the room now.

"If all of this could solve every one of my problems, I'd be happy," said Frederik quietly.

'But we have to dance, to spin and to enjoy the kiss of the death fairy. Come on, darling, kiss me.' The demon danced and sung on an invisible vine in front of Frederik's eyes, which were closed for a long dream.

✦

I knew from the beginning that not everyone could be innocent in a group of so many special people. I was happy the crazy one confessed before he was unconscious. He remained the weakest in the group for me. I investigated everything without Ralph's help, and I managed to solve a case which was three years old. I almost arrested Frederik, who had killed the girl as well. However, he was in the crazy house, and I knew it'd be hard to convict him from there.

All evidence for blackmailing was there and obvious for the judge as well. My boss should be happy with me for now and Ralph could just go back to the passport control.

The investigations were closed really quickly, and I was sure the press would write something about my efficiency in the next paper. I wanted to finish the protocol before I could finally go to bed and forget all about those weird people. Spitting fire, eating knives and hypnotists are just not the right company for me.

Ms Hiersemann was even ruder to me than she normally was. Another result of the bad influence of Ralph. I thought she'd correct him; however, she seemed to be interested in him.

'Sleaze ball,' I thought when I saw how he used his big, brown eyes with Ms Hiersemann. And she looked like a stupid, silly girl, coquetting around him like this! She should be ashamed because of how old she was.

'Old trout!' Sorry, it was just on my mind.

When I checked the papers of one of the earlier investigations, I found mistakes by my colleagues. I now wanted to note them down and correct them. Sloppiness like this should have internal consequences.

The first thing everyone forgot about was the costume, which wasn't torn after all. Young Benny checked it thoroughly and Helene approved. The change of positions, also approved by Helene, was another thing no one wrote down. Those officers should have noticed that it was only Elmira, Natalia and Frederik who were able to climb up the alignment.

One sloppy piece of work after another. I was just happy I didn't have to deal with someone from Munich who thought they were something better than me.

I had already finished more than two pages when I realised that Ralph was still around.

When I thought he had finally gone, he came into my office, holding another folder in his hand.

"Vingard, here's something we have to talk about."

"I'm sorry, but as I told my boss, I don't need any help and you can just go back to where you came from." I thought I had ended the conversation so I could go back to my work.

"I don't care if you're all right with it or not, but Frederik cannot be Natalia's murderer. The fact that he was responsible for Elmira's accident was something I told you even before you started the interviews. It would've been nice if you had told your boss about it as well," he complained. But I acted nonchalantly and just ignored him.

"I have to write my report. See you."

"You can't write it, as the murderer is missing. You have to open the old case again."

"Oh please. How could you know? He was at the station, alone and unattended. His wife couldn't agree or deny it as she was out shopping. He's strong enough to strangle someone. What else do you want?" Kicking him would've probably been more effective for Ralph to decide to leave me alone finally. He had changed from being the nice colleague into the lead investigator and I didn't like it at all.

"Frederik didn't need a strap from the trapeze to hold on to the vines. He can climb without any accessories. You should've asked Earl Rasnov. Those ropes in the theatre are obviously the murder weapon. They don't really look very unusual, so I think they're rubbish more than anything else. But the perpetrator must have some marks on their hand. Frederik didn't have any. He's trembling too much, and his skin became very brittle because of his medication. You should've seen it when you questioned him. I saw it as soon as he entered the room with his nurse," concluded Ralph.

I had to admit it, the boy was good. Maybe I should've listened to him.

"So, what do you say? Who's the murderer?"

✦

Ralph's arguments convinced me, and Vingard seemed happy with his colleague as well, although he was still slightly jealous. It seemed like the hostility between them had not been solved yet.

Everyone from the acting group came back to the inn and the office in Garmisch was as good as empty. Only Vingard and Ralph were left in the kitchen and tried to work together. All lights were off, and the cleaners were gone as well.

"I don't know what I did for you to treat me like this. It's not long ago since you asked me to help you," complained Ralph.

"Let's concentrate on the only thing which connects the two of us. What else did you find out?" Vingard acted as if it was a strictly professional conversation and avoided every personal topic.

"Can you tell me why you're having such a hard time with this group?" Ralph was curious, but he also wanted to relax his colleague.

"They don't fit here and they're just different. I think I'm simply too uncomfortable talking to people like them. I'm not a big-city guy, but that's not in the way of this investigation, is it?" For one moment too long, Vingard looked at Ralph before he abruptly turned his head around.

"Of course not. You just make it harder for yourself. I don't have any experience in investigations like these, but I seem to be better at handling people, no matter where they're from or what they're like. Are you convinced that both deaths are connected?" Ralph seemed to continue to be polite, despite the bad mood Vingard was in. It acted as some kind of bridge between both men. Vingard walked around in the room to stretch his legs for a bit. He looked at the tables around him, which seemed to be invisible in the darkness.

"Without a doubt. Earl Rasnov himself should've come to us earlier. He wanted to investigate himself and now he's scared to be responsible for Natalia's death," said Vingard.

He sat at the table again and looked at his report.

"Frederik's on three times the number of pills which the doctor told him to take. I asked his wife to come here. I have an appointment with her at nine o'clock tomorrow." Ralph handed out the protocol of the conversation between Frederik and his doctor.

Vingard looked up and wondered how he could have missed such a detail.

"I thought about calling his doctor as well," he lied.

"Good. We saved a bit of work there. The doctor confirmed Frederik's disorientation. It's partly because of the side effects of his medication, which was too high. He wasn't able to do something like this. He also said that Frederik couldn't sit at the train station alone. He needed constant care. I asked if Frederik would be able to perform in the show, as this is the reason why he is here anyway." Ralph paused. He wasn't sure if Vingard was listening to him.

"Yes, continue. I can only see the statement of that Spanish woman here," said Vingard slightly absently.

"Well, the doctor said there shouldn't be any problems with a normal dose of neuroleptics, but Frederik has to go to rehab first. He said his colleague might have overlooked the earlier prescriptions and given him more of his medication than needed. However, he said that'd be a harmless mistake. I don't believe him though. What did you read there?" asked Ralph.

"I'm sure we did the right thing by pressuring Frederik. He said earlier already that he was responsible for Elmira's death. His wife said it was because of his trauma, but I'm sure she was just messing with us. It's a good thing you asked her to come here tomorrow. Now we should go home as well. Enough work for today."

The last light in the office went out and the two men went separate ways home. They left behind the beginning of a new way towards a bridge no one could see.

✦

The door of the elevator opened, and a woman stepped into the entrance hall at exactly nine o'clock. She wore an elegant green costume made out of a heavy fabric and her hair was pinned up traditionally, just like a Bavarian woman. I barely realised that this was the actor Bianca, as she looked very tired this morning. Suddenly, it looked like she had aged significantly. It seemed like she had lost some of her grace.

Inspector Vingard still wasn't speaking to me. I was determined to look for a new job after this case was done. I wouldn't want to work on another case with the railway police. It was exciting, but to wait for the evil and to find it seemed to cause trouble which I didn't want to have in my life.

The victim didn't seem to be a good person, but I couldn't ever just accept her death. I got up and went to Bianca. Her eyes were very red, and her cheeks seemed pale.

"Thank you for coming," I said politely, but I tried to remain professional. I was still part of this investigation and I wanted to do a good job until it was completely over.

"What's this about?" We went to the meeting room.

"Bianca. We have to talk about why your husband is on so many drugs. I think you know about Frederik's statement from yesterday. But it's only with your help that we can finally close this case. And we want our doctors to check your hands." She nodded. I signalled to Ms Hiersemann to help out as a registrar. We had only known each other for a short period of time, however, we liked each other very much. She told me about how she didn't like Inspector Vingard. That was the first thing we had in common.

"You do not have to say anything, but anything you do say may be given in evidence and if you don't tell us the truth it'll be obstruction of justice. Do you understand?" Bianca nodded.

"Vingard, do you want me …?" I started. "No, there's no need for it. I can protocol it myself." I answered myself and Ms Hiersemann sat down next to me.

"I think I know what will follow now. I don't want to cause more stress here. It was almost three years ago, when I caught my husband having sex with Natalia in the wardrobe. My husband had sex with every girl and every woman in the group. He was good looking and shortly after our marriage, I made peace with the fact that he'd never be just my man. I gave up any claim to fidelity or monogamy from the beginning." Bianca quickly opened her handbag and got out a tissue. She looked resigned and her trembling hands indicated the recent sleepless nights she'd had.

"It was two weeks later when Natalia called Frederik right before one of our shows. She told him that she was pregnant. He asked her to have an abortion. He wouldn't leave me, nor would he take on the responsibility for a child. That's what he told me later, anyway."

Ms Hiersemann and I were interested in what she said, however, so far, we knew most of it already.

"When Natalia didn't agree to having an abortion, Frederik tried to make her take emergency contraception. He hid it in a praline. It's silly, but sometimes even the easiest tasks are too much for men. Natalia was crazy for chocolate. Unfortunately, my husband is not the best perpetrator, and Natalia caught him. Since then, Natalia blackmailed us as she apparently kept the pill to prove we wanted to poison her. During this time, Natalia had more financial difficulties and she asked for more and more money off us."

Ms Hiersemann quickly noted all of this down and looked at the glass wall, to check if Inspector Vingard was still around.

"When Pavel told us about Natalia lying to Otto as well, we immediately knew that she just wanted money and that her pregnancy was just faked. It was just obvious for us that she was a traitor. I told Pavel about my idea of getting the invoices from her doctor. I also said that it was just an idea and that he could say it was his. I didn't want to hurt his pride. He's very sensitive about it."

I didn't know anything about situations like these, and I wanted to ask Vingard to come inside, but he looked like he was still busy celebrating his alleged victory.

"When I asked Natalia about it, I told her that she'd never see any of our money again, she told me that the light on the stage was meant to hit her and that she knew about it. That's why she changed her position with Elmira. Frederik didn't want to hit Elmira, but he wanted to scare Natalia. Frederik told me about it a few months later. Since then, he was haunted by weird thoughts. That's the reason why I upped his dose of pills. He seemed to have thought of getting help by his friends himself. Earl Rasnov managed to convince him to go to hospital. If the truth were to have come out, we would've lost everything. But we did lose it all now anyway," said Bianca who couldn't hold back her tears anymore. We waited for her to stop crying.

Ms Hiersemann handed her a box of tissues and looked at me.

"When she called me to ask why she was supposed to be in Eschenlohe by eight, I thought about why she'd think that. It was later when I saw her invitation. She ripped something off it without noticing. That's why I met her on the train at seven a.m. when we were still in Munich."

'Oh my God,' I said to myself.

"Why did Natalia call you?" asked my colleague.

"She said that Benny told her we'd both be picked up in Eschenlohe at the same time. But silly as she was, she didn't understand the time properly. Somehow she managed to miss the one in front of the eight on the invitation."

"What happened next?" I asked.

"I asked her to come to the toilets, so I could give her the money for her trip and stay here in Eschenlohe. She believed what I said and when I had the chance to, I took the leather strap from her luggage, put it around her throat and strangled her."

Bianca realised Ms Hiersemann and I were surprised.

"I had to protect my husband. Natalia would've never shut up. She wanted to expose Frederik in front of Earl Rasnov. She wanted to tell him that Frederik was responsible for Elmira's death. But it was an accident!"

"Accident? Damn it! You strangled a woman and glossed over the accident your husband caused. You're really understating here. Still, you have to be checked by our doctor."

She nodded and cried. I had to gasp for air.

'This job is not for me,' I had to conclude.

Da Capo

Ralph gave up his job at the railway police. After the rehab, they arrested Frederik and he was still waiting for his trail. It wouldn't be easy for him as his pills caused a lot of damage. I heard that he apparently became even more crazy and talked to himself now.

Ms Hiersemann addressed many reproaches after Ralph quit. She even went to my boss and told them all about it. It really wasn't a fun case. Not just because of the horrible payment, but because of all the stress I had with my colleagues. I almost left as well.

It was barely one month after Bianca confessed to all of it, when Ralph visited me with a massive smile on his face. He told me about being Benny's successor in the group now. I suppose he fitted in well with … those … people.

I needed more than two weeks to document this case and Ms Hiersemann asked me every day to change something else on it.

All the actors have been rehearsing for several weeks now in Murnau. They'll have their premiere in Munich in two weeks. I was surprised when I received an invitation for it.

I want to take some time off and actually go and see it.

Frederik's wife Bianca confessed everything and told us exactly how Natalia had blackmailed them. In the end, even we hated Natalia. However, we can't judge ourselves. It was surprising to me, coming from a woman of her age and shape, but somewhere I suppose I could understand it.

Helene was busy in Berlin and told me shortly after the confession that she moved there. Apparently, people praised her there as a big artist. It was all over social media that she received a prize for the best costume. I never thought she had it in her. She was always very monosyllabic and always seemed slightly crazy. Not really like a woman who was about to have a massive career on the stage.

'But what do I know?' I asked myself very seriously.

The husband and his giant had a luxurious party in Murnau. There was a lot of press and stars. It was on the news for almost two weeks.

Pavel didn't speak very highly of me during almost every interview he gave.

I definitely developed a lot from meeting his group and Ralph. However, I didn't have the urge to experience anything like it again.

I booked a hotel very close to the dance school in Munich and I hope I get the chance to talk to Ralph about our success.

There was a lot about this case that was still on my mind, and I still couldn't really understand what had actually happened. It was like everything was planned for me for Bianca and Frederik to confess. Both of them were almost forced to confess, but I think: all's well that ends well. I don't want to think about it anymore.

The old Earl never spoke to me again. I didn't get an invitation to his engagement party either. I bet Ralph will be there to present his puppy eyes, so he'll get all the compliments.

'Arsehole,' I swore mentally.

I never really understood him. I was so excited about him when we met. I wished we were brothers or could at least have spent more time together. However, everything made me feel so uncomfortable, I just pushed him away.

I don't know why I did it, and I hope I didn't make a massive fool out of myself.

I miss him.

✦

I was looking forward to my last day of work. Since I realised that my training in the police doesn't fulfil my personal goals, it forced me to change something. I almost cried when Earl Rasnov asked me to be part of his group.

Vingard has been blaming himself for several weeks now and I can't look at his apologies anymore. If I counted correctly, it was his twenty-second email in which he mentioned the bad phase he was in right now.

'Bad for him,' I thought.

I can call Ms Hiersemann Margot now and she'll come to my premiere.

I learned how to use my knowledge of weapons in our shows. I'm the Ghost-rider. I ride a motorbike on stage and shoot things like clay pigeons and flying targets. Some of my shots are just faked. I use a children's gun and Benny shoots my blanks in the installations room. My costume was designed by an Italian. Pavel bought his clothes there and somehow persuaded him to join the group.

There was one of Vingard's emails that I worried about. It was true that all the confessions and coincidences in this case were very exceptional. It was almost too easy. Everything was just made for Frederik and Bianca to confess. But the question Vingard asked made me remember something I learned in my former profession.

'Was it just Bianca and Frederik who confessed or was Natalia sentenced to death?' asked Vingard.

When I spent more time with Earl Rasnov and his son Benny, I realised that I was surrounded by great strategists here. Benny was highly intelligent, and Earl Rasnov knew how to act around people.

We would never be able to prove if it was planned like this or not. There was one detail I asked for, which Vingard couldn't explain to me.

I asked if Natalia's invitation was in her bag. I saw it during the trial in one of the files, and there really was the number one missing on her invitation. Apparently, she ripped this bit off; however, no one ever found it. Everyone thought she must've thrown it away.

"Why did you not invite everyone via email?" I asked Benny a few weeks ago.

"My father always wants to be very distinguished. Invitations via email are definitely forbidden. It's the same for birthday wishes and condolence cards," he explained.

I stopped asking.

Virginia moved in with Ignez a few weeks ago. As Benta had her engagement party coming up, she apparently wanted Ignez to announce that she now shares a home with Virginia. Ignez didn't want to co-operate, but she couldn't take issue with her mother.

A lot of different artists praised Pavel and Otto for getting married. Other than with the 'Bloody soirée,' they were busy with a lot of TV interviews. It looks like their experience with Natalia's death will soon be topic of a TV show as well.

I am now moving from Garmisch to Murnau for good. During the time we perform the 'Bloody soirée' in Munich, I'll live in Otto and Pavel's guestroom.

My make-up has started melting already and I'm a nervous wreck. I'll now put everything together on my social media account before I go on stage. We rehearsed for weeks and now the premiere has come.

In case I have a breakdown or shoot myself by accident, I at least have everything put together in one place.

Okay, the engine is running.

"Pavel, get the fire going!"

✦

According to the press, the premier of the 'Bloody soirée' was very successful. Pavel, artist of fire and light, enchanted the audience with his opening. He was dressed as Earl Drago from a so-far unknown designer Pietro Venolini and finished under the direction of Helene Mourad. She will receive an award for her beautiful stage project of 'The Castle in the Valley' in Berlin. Although she separated herself from Earl Rasnov's group, she is still sad because of the good times they had together. She followed her career and moved to Berlin.

That's why Ignez Hierro planned the stage design of the 'Bloody soirée'. She was part of the show as well. She showed us during the opening with Pavel what a fiery flamenco dancer can look like as well.

There was an article in the local section for Eschenlohe about the landlady of the inn. She published a photo spread of the group of actors, which shows how she survived living in the inn with a murderer under her roof. Some of her pictures showed her, together with her Asian waiter, dressed in typical Bavarian dress. What stood out in those pictures was the landlady looking quite shocked, whereas her assistant had a massive smile on her face.

Rumour has it that Ignez Hierro moved in with the knife-thrower and Olympian champion in biathlon, Virginia Giebitz. Together they're now head of the dance school in Munich which, thanks to the 'Bloody soirée,' has had many new applications. The waiting time is at least four weeks. The dance school is considered to be an absolute success in Munich and stars love spending their time there.

It would've been easy to miss the only bad press about this show. Two stagehands from Murnau complained about the tough and excruciating work they had to do for Earl Rasnov. They reported many brutalities of his hard leadership and wanted to sue him. There was no information about the reason for their complaint and no pictures of the two workers, who were already under notice to leave.

All this news was part of an old newspaper, which an old man picked up as he was collecting bottles at the train station in Eschenlohe.

When he finished it, he scrunched it up, threw it in the bin and hoped to see those artists again next year.

✦

Further publications of this author

German Romans

- Altreia, Drama, 1998
- Geheimnis der verdorrten Rosen, Mystery, 2009 – Reimo Verlag *
- Virtuelle Liebe, Kurzroman, Thriller, 2016 *
- Paloma, Kurzroman, Thriller, 2016 *
- Die Muse, Kurzroman, Erzählung, 2016 *
- Post-mortem Kino, Roman, Drama, 2016 *
- Die Heilerin, Roman, Thriller, 2017 *
- Geheimnis der verdorrten Rosen, Mystery, 2017 (neue Version) *
- Der Zauberspiegel des Eros, Roman, Thriller, 2017 *
- Das Tal, Roman, Thriller, 2017 *
- Jahreszeiten der Sünde, Roman, Thriller, 2018 *
- Sein letztes Opfer, Roman, 2020 *
- Wieland, der Schmied, Volksheldensage, 2020 *

English Romans

- Virtual Affairs, 2018 *
- Paloma, 2019 *
- Earl Rasnov's Bloody Soiree, 2019 *

German Radio Novels and Comics

- Roberta, 2020
- Die Muse, 2019
- Paloma, 2018
- Virtuelle Liebe, 2017

Kunstkataloge

- Geliebter Vater, 1995 *
- The new Artist, 1996 und 1997
- Liebe in Stücken, 2009 *
- Kunstkatalog, 2010
- Liebe in Stücken, Edition II, 2016 *
- Kunstkatalog, 2017 *
- Kunstkatalog, 2018 *
- Kunstkatalog, 2019 *
- Kunstkatalog – The man inside 2020 *

(*) Listed

Thank you, to everyone who took time for my research.